25 Famous African Folktales

Mauritz Mostert

Published by Wildmoz, 2020.

Table of Contents

....1

COPYRIGHT 2

PREFACE...3

CHAPTER 1 4

THE GREAT ANIMAL BATTLE 5

CHAPTER 2 17

HOW THE ZEBRA GOT HIS STRIPES 18

CHAPTER 3 30

HOW GIRAFFE STRETCHED HIS NECK..............31

CHAPTER 4 36

THE CHIEF, THE SUITOR AND THE KENGE.......37

CHAPTER 5 44

THE SAN AND THE GREAT STORM 45

CHAPTER 6 63

HOW ELEPHANT AND WARTHOG GOT THEIR TUSKS.........64

CHAPTER 7 68

BLINDMAN AND HUNCHBACK...........................69

CHAPTER 8 85

SNAKE AND THE YOUNG MAN 86

CHAPTER 9 91

HOW THE LEOPARD GOT HIS SPOTS.................92

CHAPTER 10...105

THE CARPENTER AND THE LEGUAAN...............106

CHAPTER 11...111

HOW MANTIS GAVE THE BUSHMAN FIRE.......112

CHAPTER 12...118

THE DAMSEL AND THE DRAGONFLY 119

CHAPTER 13...127

JACKAL, LION AND THE FALLING ROCKS.......128

CHAPTER 14...131

THE CHIEF WHO WAS NO FOOL 132

CHAPTER 15...145

THE MOUSE AND THE LION 146

CHAPTER 16...152
WHY CHEETAH'S CHEEKS ARE STAINED.....................................153
CHAPTER 17...157
HYENA, LION AND SQUIRREL...158
CHAPTER 18...162
THE KIND-HEARTED HUNTER...163
CHAPTER 19...182
HOW HIPPO LOST HIS HAIR..183
CHAPTER 20...190
MONKEY'S FIDDLE AND BOW...191
CHAPTER 21...201
THE MOUTHFUL OF MIRACLES..202
CHAPTER 22...208
WHY WARTHOG WALKS ON HIS KNEES....................................209
CHAPTER 23...211
JABU AND THE LION..212
CHAPTER 24...227
HOW CHEETAH BECAME SO FAST..228
CHAPTER 25...231
LEOPARD, RAM AND JACKAL..232
THE END...238

25 FAMOUS AFRICAN FOLKTALES

Mauritz Mostert

EDITOR

Cari Mostert

COPYRIGHT

PREFACE

25 Famous African Folktales, not called famous for nothing. African Folktales are common to most of the tribes and peoples of Africa. Different cultures, whilst sharing a common point of reference, will colour each story with their own rich, unique heritage. These tales by tradition were handed down by word of mouth through the ages, to be enjoyed by young and old alike.

Honouring tradition, I tried to keep the "voice" of the original storytellers of old, in the same manner in which they spoke, centuries ago. Contractions have been left out, since they were not the mode of speech in those bygone days.

In Africa, myths and tall tales abound, around the next mountain, through yonder valley, you will find a story that almost sounds the same as one you heard before. Thus, there are many versions of each tale. I believe my stories capture the essence of originality, having been adapted from traditional oral folktales.

Many folktales about Africa inspired countless expeditions in search of mysteries and treasures, from golden mountains, to lost tribes, to amazing animals. How did they get there? How were they made? Were they kind or fierce? Were they friendly or terrifying? Yes, some were gentle, some were vicious, but all had a story to tell. Who are they? What do they stand for, what nature do they have?

All beings possess traits of one kind or another, which are discovered in folktales.

These stories have been built upon ancient traditions. As an African-born author, I owe a debt of gratitude to all our ancestors who passed down wonderful fables and tales, from which these stories are derived. It is to them, I dedicate my books.

CHAPTER 1

THE GREAT ANIMAL BATTLE

Long, long, ago somewhere in Africa, when all the people and animals were new. The darkest day in Africa started something like this.

Here, beginning at the beginning, at what was said to be the beginning, we do not know, because no one knows. Yet one thing we do know is the animal kingdom was still in its infancy, so as to say.

The quest for sovereignty between the Things-of-the-Earth and the Things-of-the-Air had been brewing for some time. The object. Dominion.

Naturally, the Things-of-the-Air claimed more special abilities than the Things-of-the-Earth, because they could fly. They asserted to possess a better understanding of the world because seeing more of it, they held a better knowledge, therefore a better education. Consequently, they claimed the best advantage from which to rule.

Hippo, an aquatic mammal, denied their claim, on the grounds that most of the Things-of-the-Air were uneducated, without any idea of matters involving creatures in the water. Of course, Crocodile, Otter and the other aquatic animals naturally agreed with him.

The-Things-of-the-Earth, on the other hand, claimed they were the true kings of the world, having lived and ruled on the Earth and what is more, without the Earth, the Things-of-the-Air would not survive. And they, The Things-of-the-Earth, were not intending to relinquish their control over the Earth any time soon.

For some time, the Things-of-the-Earth and the Things-of-the-Air vied with one another for absolute control, but never in a grand way. Each group believed their powers and qualities superior to any other, lifting themselves above the rest in stature and position, thereby claiming the highest status among all the animals.

This self-aggrandizement was bringing derision to every animal throughout Africa. It was obvious to see the leaders of the clans, herds, pods, flocks, convocations, crashes, bands, parades —you know what I mean—were the guilty ones. It was they, who were the main protagonists in the quarrels and do not forget their supporters. But of course, when push came to shove, no one would admit they were to blame. An important thing to understand is the clans, herds, flocks, bands, etcetera, etcetera and so on, were still small at this time.

ANTAGONIST, PROTAGONIST

EARLY ONE SUMMER MORNING, in their typical fashion, a venue of vultures came to gather on the branches of an old dead tree, above where Lion, Jackal and Hyena were resting. Obviously choosing to be in earshot, on purpose, Bald Vulture, bragging again true to character, addressed Black Vulture.

"I must say, I think I have eaten more Things-of-the-Earth than any other bird alive."

"Never mind bird, I think you may have eaten even more than Lion, Hyena and Jackal put together."

Lion was unimpressed with these vultures talking about him in this way, especially in his presence. He allowed them to rile him, letting them get under his skin, thereby falling right into their trap.

"Listen, you, black air pig, if I challenged you, you would simply fly away like a chicken-hearted escape artist. You only eat the dead you steal, where others kill. Your talk is big, but your heart is yellow. You are not even brave enough to back up your mouth in your own defence. As for you, you devious, bald, scavenging carcass percher, come down here and fight. How dare you come to bother peaceful creatures like us, minding our own business?"

This is how the animals would speak to one another. Why they became this way is anyone's guess, but it was this nature that led to that dark day of the big battle.

All of a sudden, as if from nowhere, birds began flooding the surrounding trees in support of the vultures.

That was it. Within seconds, no one could hear themselves think, the air simply awash with screeching birds. Some of the Things-of-the-Earth shouted back, except Lion, who covered his ears with his paws.

In the cacophony, the most noticeable was Jackal yowling in frustration, backed by Hyena's incessant cackling. At the same time, he jumped up snapping at the birds. Both were challenged by Go'way bird, feathers on end in disarray, screaming himself drunk with passion, craning out his neck as he squawked, spitting out purple berry pips in all directions. As if the din was not enough, Hornbill joined in the parade at Go'way's side, adding his discordant notes to the already highly charged atmosphere.

Martial Eagle, largest of the eagles and leader of the Things-of-the-Air shouted above the din.

"Enough! You talk too much. Dive, dive, straight for the eyes, make your blows count, all of you."

Black Eagle could not wait, diving through the crowd-filled tree, with Crow in hot pursuit headed straight for Jackal. Now on the run, Jackal streaked for safety, any safety. Black Eagle struck first, taking a big bite out of his right ear, while Crow pecked away at his rear-end. Jackal screamed his head off.

"I am dead! I am dead! I am dead!"

And, scrambling for his life, he dived into the nearest Aardvark hole. Martial Eagle almost got a Lion's paw straight to the face, while he narrowly escaped being downed by the other paw.

CAUGHT WITHOUT WARNING

THE FIRST ONSLAUGHT by the Things-of-the-Air caught the Things-of-the-Earth by surprise, scattering them near and far. Lion roared to call order to his assembly, shaking the ground till even the trees lost some seeds, bringing leaves fluttering down. Lion motioned for them all to gather around. The whole mess was working on Lion's sense of decorum, rattling his nerves.

"This is chaos. If there is going to be a battle, there must be order. Eagle, what are your thoughts?"

"I believe a battle someday is unavoidable. Therefore, to my mind, this day is as good a day as any."

"Well said. In that case, we are in need of umpires, or else we will never know how the fight is progressing, or who wins. We must set rules, to which both sides must strictly adhere. Insects are not part of this fight, because they are not all identifiable as flying, crawling, creeping, jumping or swimming creatures. Many start out as crawlers, then get to fly, so what are they? Therefore, the umpires must keep a lookout for those too. First, who will be the umpire for the Things-of-the-Air?"

Martial Eagle wasted no time in his umpire's nomination.

"From my side, I nominate Ostrich. He is tall, strong and honest as the day is long."

"I am most certainly a noble of the bird family, yet fly, I cannot, where does that place me, O Lion, amongst the ones of the air or of the ground?"

Hearing pedantic old Ostrich, Jackal, never short of something to say, even though mostly not complementary or useful, was grinning from ear to ear and not able to help himself piped up.

"Come, three sticks, chase me. If you go quickly enough, you can open your wings, then dive, this way we will find out. Keep close, I will tell you when."

This made Ostrich hopping mad, roaring like a lion, he menacingly ran straight for Jackal, waltzing, darting, wings outstretched. With Jackal zig-zagging and ducking every which way. Unable to shake off his assailant, he dived straight for cover, escaping right under Lion for protection, bringing raucous laughter to all the bystanders.

"Tuck your feet up and fly you clumsy bird."

Lion called order again, scowling at Jackal, suggesting Ostrich was the perfect candidate for the Things-of-the-Air. Martial Eagle approved. Lion continued.

"You, Ostrich, will stand on the hilltop on the left alongside this valley. There you will hold your head up high, when you see your kind are winning, then lower it when they are losing. That brings us to a representative for the Things-of-the-Earth."

Many stepped forward. But once again, it was Jackal who made the most fuss, suggesting he would be the best candidate. Still holding his head to one side, pointing out the bad wound Black Eagle gave him, to anyone who would look.

"No one will do a better job than I."

Lion was the most sceptical.

"What makes you think this is the job for you, Jackal? This is a job more suited to Giraffe."

"You must keep Giraffe. He can see far and wide, to warn of approaching danger. Everyone is quite able to see me on the top of that big anthill, which Giraffe cannot climb anyway. I will hold my silvery gold tail up high, where it will glisten in the sun for all to see. If you are losing, I will drop it down. Besides, I am wounded, so not fit for fighting duty."

Lion thought it over, realizing it may be better to select Jackal, knowing his nature to run at the first sign of danger.

"I think Jackal is right, besides if one begins to run, which I think he will, many will follow endangering all the rest. Let it be so Jackal. It is you who will be our umpire, also to you, as I said to Ostrich, you must strictly obey the rules. If I, at any time, find you cheating, you will have to deal with me."

From on top of a small kopje, Lion assisted by Martial Eagle, ironed out the rules together, in the presence of the umpires and many bystanders. Soon as all was done, both umpires went to take up their respective positions.

LAYING OUT THE BATTLEFIELD

WHILE THE THINGS-OF-the-Earth were laying out their battlefield, Lion with his compatriots passed by the river where Hippopotamus and Crocodile were awaiting their instructions.

"Because you Crocodile, are unpredictable, no one in their right mind would turn their back on you. I suggest you stay in the river to defend it. As for you Hippo, I also think since you with yours, know the ways of Crocodile with his, it would be best you help one another with the Otters at your sides to save the river from a take-over."

Lion passing on by the river went about setting his troops by their respective family groups. He positioned them in an array across the valley, facing the Things-of-the-Air. In the front line, were placed the many cat families like Leopard, Lynx and Cheetah, along with the many dog families like Hyena, Wild Dog and Wolf on either side of himself. They were considered the bravest of all the Things-of-the-Earth.

Behind them came the swiftest gazelles with the antelope of the plains like Springbuck, Zebra, Wildebeest and Oryx first. After these, the antelope of the forests like Kudu, Impala, Bushbuck and Sable. Behind them in turn, Lion set the ape families like Gorilla, Chimpanzee, Baboon and Monkey. These possessed agile movements, ones who could duck, dive and jump high. Reasoning, they would disrupt the Things-of-the-Air from getting too close to those in the front or the back of his troops.

In-between these, he placed the smaller of the Earth's animal kingdom, like Porcupine, Warthog, Badger Aardvark, Mongoose and Meerkat to serve mainly as messengers, to support the entire force. He set the heavyweights like Elephant, Rhino, Buffalo, Eland, Camel and Giraffe in the rear. His thinking being, none would run away if they were to go through the giants at the back. This mass stretched across the valley from hillside to hillside. Then Lion gave a stern warning.

"My friends, guard your eyes at all times."

Martial Eagle was master and commander of the Things-of-the-Air. He also set his forces in the trees, arrayed over the valley, matching his troops in the manner in which he saw Lion set out his fighters. Martial Eagle noticed the agile ape families in the middle of Lion's forces. Warning the larger of his birds like Secretary, Marabou Stalk, Ground Hornbill, along with their kind, to keep clear of the apes. Eagle directed the vultures, especially the huge Bald and Bearded Vultures and the like, to mainly attack the rear, keeping away from the middle ground. The Eagle families, like himself, he instructed to strike the front troops beyond the cats and dogs.

Swift flyers, like Falcon, Hawk, Crow, Woodpecker, Buzzard, the Plover family with his friends and the Shrikes, were assigned the middle ground of Lion's troops. There they could strike fast and get out quickly. Martial Eagle strictly instructed his forces to attack from out of the sun at all times, heading for the eyes.

"Blind animals cannot fight back."

Imagine two of the most formidable animal forces in living memory, about to engage in a 'spare-no-life' war, a fate Africa had been spared, till this terrible day.

When the attack signal was given by Ostrich and Jackal, a new irreversible chapter in history commenced for life in Africa, destined to change her forever.

It was obvious. All had abandoned any thought for the future. No one was caring about their future offspring, or about the developing animal kingdom. If any of their species were to survive, something momentous was needed to happen and quickly. What would stop this determination for destruction they all possessed right then for each other? No one was considering survival or the cost of their possible annihilation.

"Follow me."

The rallying cry of Martial Eagle echoed far and wide across the skies over Death Valley. The birds following their leader, attacked in one great cloud. A mighty destructive force of screaming feathers dived earthwards with the sun at their backs, immediately obscuring a once glistening blue sky.

It was no surprise to see Ostrich extending his head up as high as his neck would allow, showing the Things-of-the-Air were winning.

Wave after wave, the Things-of-the-Air kept coming. For some time, dust and carnage reigned supreme throughout the valley with the sickening stench of death in the air. But the war went on. In all the pandemonium, it was hard to make out what was, or was not going on.

Sadly Jackal, fearing for his kind, decided to put his tail up high in the air to show the Things-of-the-Earth had begun to win for the first time. A confused Ostrich, seeing his opponent high above the dust with tail pointing skyward, assumed the better part of valour would be to lower his head. As a result, Eagle's forces scattered in all directions for safety.

Go'way came to perch alongside Martial Eagle as they landed. Ignoring his compatriot's chirping, Eagle was observing the disarray of his troops. Go'way was complaining that Jackal was cheating, which he believed to be the cause of the big mess-up. Go'way, making a quick trip over to talk to Ostrich, went ahead to prove his point to Eagle. When Eagle, still listening with one ear, realized Jackal was the culprit and perpetrator of his dilemma, he came to his senses, tout suite. Not wasting a moment, he called for retaliation against Jackal.

In the meantime, after seeing the opposition fly away and observing Jackal's clear signal sporting his tail high up in the air, Lion's troops regathered, ready for the next onslaught.

This was not good for the Things-of-the-Air, having fought so hard to get to where they were. Martial Eagle, fuming, looked around to find who he should send to execute his judgment against Jackal.

"Hadeda, find me a giant wasp. I have a mission for him."

After a short while, Hadeda returned, followed by Wasp hot on his tail, coming to rest next to Eagle. Eagle, whispering to Wasp, giving careful instructions on what he wanted him to do, without anyone hearing.

"Wait, I cannot do that. What if Lion finds out? I and my kind will be wiped out from the face of the Earth for cheating."

"Never mind Lion, Jackal is paying for what he has sown, therefore I will take responsibility."

Wasp, realizing there being many witnesses, was satisfied, proud to be able to serve the cause of the Things-of-the-Air with honour. He embarked on his mission. Round he went, out of Jackal's sight, doing as Martial Eagle commanded, stinging Jackal right in the there-after.

Instantly, letting out a blood-curdling scream, Jackal fled across the valley, making a bee-line straight for the river, diving headfirst into the water, forgetting all about the dangers of Crocodile.

JUDGEMENT

A CRY WENT UP FROM the Things-of-the-Earth, seeing Jackal disappear into the waters of the river. But, before anyone found out what happened, a strange scene appeared in the sky, accompanied by a deathly silence.

Seemingly from nowhere, there appeared a dust storm, obliterating the distant horizon, spanning Death Valley from side to side. While sweeping across the battlefield, intimidating darkness from the rapidly-approaching upper clouds covered the Earth.

Crashing down from over the mountains, it came. Thumping into the ground at the bottom end of the valley, sending electrical currents crackling through the air, generating streaks of lightning as it hit the valley floor. Aching from raised fur or feathers, all watched in paralyzed terror. Groaning loudly as it went, the storm rumbled up the valley, eating up the ground, heading directly for the defenceless battle array, huddled and rooted together.

Closely behind, flashing ceaseless blinding lightning and ear-shattering thunder, came the storm, with torrents of ice-cold rain and hail. Then the ground began to shake, like a massive beaten drum. It shook so hard the Things-of-the-Earth wobbled on their feet, stumbling as they walked. When some managed to get their footing, they ran for their lives. Fleeing for cover, any cover, to escape the destruction about to befall them. Birds flew in every direction, crashing into one another. Confusion reigned supreme through Earth and sky. Then panic became the order of the day.

Where that strange storm came from, no one knows, but great fear was in it. A fear it was said, no animal ever experienced before, a fear so terrible, many, in the animal kingdom thought they had lost their minds.

Blackening the sky in thick darkness, the freezing storm raged on through the day and into the night. When the morning light appeared over the rise, the tempest was gone, as if it had never been. The flaming tongues of an African sunrise blazed the way to a new day.

From a hole in the plains, the first to emerge was Lion, then from the craggy heights of the mountains came Martial Eagle. On the banks of the Great Blood River, running the length of Death Valley, was where the Things-of-the-Earth and the Things-of-the-Air met to make their truce.

"My friend Eagle, I think we must see reason here. I believe we must never again think of fighting one another, or this will definitely happen again."

"Yes, Lion, we may easily have changed the course of the animal kingdom forever. We are both too powerful to allow such a thing to be repeated. I, for one, do not want to see a storm like that ever again."

On this sad day, it is said, many in the animal kingdom vanished forever. Who they were is now lost in time?

The mysteries of Africa abound, yet a long-time lesson was learned from this battle, which has never been forgotten. Animal pride and arrogance were killed that day, leading to the harmony of one Great Animal Kingdom, with a place for everyone and everyone in their place.

The moral of the story, you say? Peace and order will overcome.

CHAPTER 2

HOW THE ZEBRA GOT HIS STRIPES

L ong, long, ago somewhere in Africa, when all the people and animals were new. There was a great drought, the sun was hot, and the water had dried from all but the deepest pans and waterholes.

Deep in the Green Desert, at one of the biggest fountain pools, was an extremely large, irritable baboon and self-proclaimed king of the Green Desert water. This baboon decided to keep the great big fountain water all to himself.

"I am Baboon king, owner of this water."

This he would declare, chasing off everyone who came that way, begging for a drink.

As is the way of the Green Desert, nights were bitterly cold, so the baboon made a big fire to keep himself warm. To never feel chilled, he kept this fire burning day and night.

Time passed, with many animals wandering to this water, pleading with the baboon for a drink, but to no avail, he chased them viciously away. All around the Green Desert grew more dusty and dry as the drought lengthened. Many animals made their way to these big sweet waters, only to be frightened away by this fire-throwing, self-proclaimed king of the water. But unbeknown to Baboon, there was one coming who did not appreciate being chased off by anyone. This was the white one called Zebra, who was well known for his courage.

Our story with Zebra began when he decided to leave the acacia country to make his home in the great, green, grassy plains of Africa. To get there, he had to pass by the big water of the Green Desert. Many of the animals, who knew of Zebra's imminent arrival, would tell the arrogant baboon king of his coming. Some said he was not far off, only days away, while others said, he was across the far side of the mountains. This they heard from Eagle, who knew of him.

"I am not afraid of anyone! I can fight, with four hands, huge teeth and I have fire! When he comes, I will show him who is the strongest king of all the kingdoms."

This the baboon king would cry in rage, stomping about throwing dust and grass into the air. Furiously, yelling his retorts to their tales of this white zebra.

In the meantime, life went on while Baboon ruthlessly chased away all the thirsty animals. He was strong and cunning, able to use his hands for throwing fiery logs at anyone who would dare to stand their ground, baring his fierce teeth, even bigger than the lion's. All in all, Baboon was a formidable foe. Both the lion and the leopard were careful of him, choosing rather to leave him alone than to start a fight.

As for Zebra, he had a long journey ahead of him to the endless grasslands, and on his way, he met many others from the animal kingdom. Now, I am going to tell you about three of these animals he met on his long journey.

ZEBRA MEETS GIRAFFE

ONE OF THE ANIMALS Zebra met at the beginning of his long journey was Giraffe. To his amazement, he had never seen such a tall animal!

"Eish"

He exclaimed, looking down at Giraffe's huge feet, then looking up, up, up, he met Giraffe's friendly brown eyes looking down at him.

"How did you get so tall and by what name do they call you?"

Zebra was trying to be polite by not asking too many questions. Although still endeavouring to remain courteous, he could not resist looking down and up once again at Giraffe's towering height.

"My name is Giraffe and my story I will tell you one day. Right now, I am on a long journey to the acacia tree country, and I am weak with thirst, in need of much water,"

"Is there no water where you have come from?"

Giraffe answered, graciously leaning down so as not to appear over lofty.

"Oh, there is plenty of water. But there the water is guarded by a great big vicious baboon, who chases everyone who goes there to drink, even using fire."

Our quietly spoken Zebra moved closer in response to Giraffe's kind gesture.

"I am going to the big plains where the large grasslands are."

"You will need water if you are going that far. On your journey, you will be crossing the Green Desert, and there is only one watering place. This is the great water claimed by the big nasty baboon,"

A solemn warning from Giraffe, continuing to lean down for him and Zebra to communicate more pleasurably.

"What is this baboon? I have never heard the name. Is he tall, strong or even like the lion?"

"Oh! No, he is not tall or like a lion, but unusually strong, with four hands, big teeth, exceptionally fast and cunning. Can jump high, climb trees, swim through water or throw things with his hands. If you know the monkey, he is like the monkey, but a lot bigger and badly behaved."

"If he is like the monkey, I am not afraid of such a one as this baboon. I will certainly take care of him when I get to this water. Also, how far is this great water?"

"Do you see those mountains over along the path you are following? A few days journey beyond them, lies the big mountains of the Green Desert, afterwards the great water."

"It seems I may have to fight this baboon, so I must be careful to keep my strength up."

"My good friend… I'll tell you a secret of the Green Desert. There are tsamma melons strewn along your way, they will sustain you, even as they have sustained me. If not for them, I surely should have died."

"What is the nature of these tsamma melons?"

Zebra, full of hopeful curiosity, knowing he may have to depend on these for some time.

"They are melons growing in the Green Desert, having a type of water inside their flesh. For me, it was difficult to sustain myself on such small fruit. I had to eat a huge quantity, but you will do well, for this is what the others are surviving on, while Baboon claims kingship of the water."

"How will I know these melons?"

"Ah, they are somewhat yellow, somewhat green, growing from long vines on the surface of the sand. Only do not eat the green ones, but choose those mostly yellow ones. They will keep your thirst at bay, although they are awfully tart and leave a thin film on your teeth."

"Giraffe, I am gratefully indebted to you for telling me this secret of these much-needed desert melons. I shall definitely look out for them along my way."

Considering Giraffe himself was chased away from the big water by Baboon. It deeply impressed him to see his acquaintance with such confidence, venturing out without so much as a murmur of concern

"You are truly brave to take on that great big brutal baboon. Further, may I enquire of your name, so I can remember you?"

"Oh, I am sorry, I never even introduced myself. The other animals call me Zebra,"

Most apologetic, feeling somewhat embarrassed, for allowing his curiosity to run away with him and in the doing, forgotten his manners.

"Ah then Zebra, I wish you a big victory over the nasty baboon, my friend. My need for water is a great one. Therefore, I must be on my way, while there is still light to travel by."

Giraffe straightened up, once more ready to continue his journey.

Zebra wished Giraffe well, telling him where the next water hole along the path was, assuring him it was not far. In this way, these two parted friends, each to their given destinies.

ZEBRA MEETS WARTHOG

FURTHER ON, WHILE AMBLING down the path deep in thought, Zebra was suddenly brought up short by a snuffling, snorting kind of sound. Right there, in front of him was the most extraordinary sight, an animal's rump protruding from the ground. All of a sudden, dirt and debris came flying out in all directions, then emerged the oddest-looking creature in Zebra's opinion anyway. Cautiously, waiting for the dust to settle, he stayed back while he stared at this bizarre vision.

Warthog, backing out of his hole in the ground, looked up in surprise to see this animal in its dazzling white coat staring at him. He was a little jealous of this sparkling apparition before him, looking down at his own hide, being, well... mostly muddy and dark. Although not so muddy these days, about which he grumbled in a gruff muttering voice, more to himself than anyone else.

Happy to see this new stranger, Warthog jumped up off his knees, introducing himself to Zebra, who in turn, did the same. Enquiring from Zebra, where he came from and where he might be going.

Zebra told him, where he had lived, what his journey involved, and of some of the animals, he met on his way. He also told him he was headed through the Green Desert, for much-needed water, from the fountain where the nasty baboon was.

Warthog, reflecting on Baboon and the water situation, told Zebra every relevant point involving this spiteful, greedy baboon's behaviour. At the same time, he happily went on rummaging in the dust, without paying the least attention to whether his guest was interested or not. Zebra could tell, the fact that Baboon had taken charge of the big water, did not please Warthog in the slightest, probably accounting for a lot of his grumpiness. In Warthog's opinion, this nasty business of Baboon must end sometime soon, for the sake of all the thirsty Green Desert animals. Disappointedly looking down at himself once more, with his not-so-muddy hide, he grumbled something under his breath.

Zebra was terribly amused by Warthog, who he thought ever so funny looking. As well as a little grumpy, on account of his nature. Warty, as Zebra liked to think of him, still kept talking away, never once looking up to see if his new friend was listening or even hearing what he said. Warty's wish, was for someone to chase that fat crazy baboon off the Green Desert forever.

In their conversation, the inevitable battle between Zebra and Baboon came up. To Warty, looking at his guest more closely, decided this matter was cut and dried. He assured Zebra he was tall and stoutly built enough to take on the big baboon and win. Zebra was grateful for Warty's support, assuring him he would do his best. Warty became happily excited, imagining the baboon chased from the Green Desert, with the water becoming free again.

Zebra could not tarry any longer with Warty, bidding him goodbye. The two had become good friends in the short time they spent together.

If we consider Zebra in his upcoming meeting with Baboon the way, Warthog looked at it. Obviously, each possessed great differences in stature, yet each had strong advantages, should it come to a fight.

Although if it came to a fight, it is good to remember, there are three things needed for victory and these Zebra possessed. First, the one in the right always has an advantage over the one in the wrong. Second, is confidence, which is a belief in one's self. Of this, Zebra was blessed with plenty. Thirdly, the most needed to succeed is courage. This, of course, Zebra possessed in abundance.

An important thing to know about Zebra was, he never troubled anyone, owing to his gentle nature, but proved a formidable foe if made angry or provoked.

ZEBRA MEETS EAGLE

ZEBRA WANDERING DOWN the track again, came upon the strangest animal, sitting on a large stump by the side of the path.

"Hello, what is your name and where are your front legs?"

"I am Eagle, who flies the skies, these are my wings, which are my arms. And your name, sir?"

Enquired he, while he proudly stretched out his huge wings, peering down closer at this strikingly white curious bystander.

'They call me Zebra. I am on my way to the great, green, grassy plains."

"Now, trouble you will certainly find on your journey to the endless grasslands because a baboon has taken control of the big water. I am the only one who can get to drink those sweet waters. Although looking at you, you look more than capable of defending yourself against many a foe. If what I have heard around is true, I think you are more than able to take care of that nasty baboon."

Declared the noble chatty Eagle, looking politely down his nose at a puzzled looking Zebra.

"Where have you heard of me?"

"I was told by the other acacia tree animals, where you come from. Seeing I can fly, it is no real distance for me."

"Oh, I see, I have heard concerning this baboon from Giraffe and Warthog, but please tell me, how then can you drink from the big water?"

"I fly down especially fast, swooping across to the other side of the water from Baboon. Quickly I take a drink there, while he jumps around shouting, throwing sand into the air, followed by burning sticks, which land short in the water."

Zebra chuckled out loud at Eagle's triumph and great self-satisfaction.

"I am sure your success must cause him much aggravation."

While getting more acquainted, Eagle shared much-needed knowledge with Zebra, till he was well-versed in matters of the Green Desert, together with Baboon's tactics. Thanks to Eagle, Zebra was now better able to understand this new world he was soon to enter. When they were ready to say their farewells, Eagle assured Zebra he would keep an eye out for his safety. Zebra was most grateful to Eagle, comforted to know his new friend would be keeping an eye over him from high in the sky.

They went their separate ways; one soaring up into the great skies with a huge cry, the other gracefully cantering on to his new destiny in the endless green grasslands.

When Zebra finally arrived at the mountains, which Giraffe told him of, he had become somewhat tired, as well as intensely thirsty.

"Where are those tsamma melons, Giraffe mentioned?"

Remarked Zebra, muttering to himself while slowly making his way across the hot sand, in the relentless desert heat. Suddenly, in a small valley, there they were, just as Giraffe told him, rambling over the sand. Immediately, he found a good-looking yellow one. Taking a huge bite to discover, it was not only full of water but also cool inside, even in this hot desert sun. These tsamma melons were not bad eating, as well as a refreshing thirst quencher. However, they were, as Giraffe said, awfully tart. Besides, they did leave a light film on the teeth, yet a true lifesaver, nonetheless.

THE BIG WATER

A FEW DAYS ON AND MANY tsamma melons later, Zebra rather dusty and a little tired, arrived at the so-called baboon king's big water, for a much-needed drink.

Baboon at this time was sitting by his fire, as was his custom towards the cool of the evening. Looking into the fire, staring at the flames, Baboon did not notice Zebra standing at a short distance watching him. Till...suddenly, his eye caught something white.

Seeing this new, unusual intruder, he jumped up barking out shouts, throwing dust into the air, to the astonishment of Zebra, who watched in amazement as Baboon danced and jumped around in front of him.

"What do you want? This is my water. I am the king of this water!"

"No, you are not. This water is for everyone."

"We will see about that. You will not drink from here. Before you try, you will have to fight me for it. Who do you think you are anyway, raiding my water?"

"My name is Zebra."

Baboon jumped back at the sound of this name, and then he froze, staring at Zebra. Instantly he remembered, here before him stood the one he had been warned of. Baboon quickly regained his composure, running straight at Zebra, screaming ear-splitting barks, he again hurled sand into the air, to frighten off his rival.

"It would be better for you to run like all the others, you stupid Zebra!"

"To fight for water is an evil thing. Although, if it must be, I am more than your match and you will have to be taught a lesson this day before the sun goes down."

Baboon's lips curled back, baring his savage teeth. In one motion, he jumped forward, grabbed a burning log from the fire, he hurled it at Zebra, who easily stepped aside unscathed.

Immediately, the fight began. Backwards, forwards, this way and that, round and round, dust everywhere. Till, with a huge kick, Zebra sent Baboon flying into the rocks of the nearby hill.

Baboon landed on his rump, with a huge thump, right on the rough rocks. So hard did he land, his rear-end was left with great, big, red, bald, patches and they are still there on his descendants to this day.

Meanwhile, Zebra unbalanced by the force of his kick, staggered into Baboon's fire, scorching his beautiful white hide, leaving him full of stripes from head to tail.

At first, when Zebra examined what happened to his pure white hide, he was pleased to find no injuries. Further inspection of his black and white reflection in the water, assured him of a handsome outlook.

First, he indulged himself in drinking his fill of the sweet water, before cooling himself off in the deep dark fountain. As he swam, he washed away his long journey's ingrained dust. Getting out, shaking himself off, he took one more look back, and satisfied with a job well done, he left. Happy to know he was leaving the waters free again for all to drink, he galloped on to the endless grasslands where he was headed from the beginning of his journey.

Unbeknown to Zebra, Eagle, high in the sky, had been watching the battle between him and Baboon.

THE GREAT AFRICAN PLAINS

WHEN ZEBRA ARRIVED at the grasslands, the other plains animals were amazed, having never seen a black and white striped creature like this before.

The grassland animals heard from Eagle how Zebra defeated Baboon, kicking him off the Green Desert.

Since Zebra overcame their enemy, making the sweet waters free again, they called a great council of the plain's animals. The council's wise decision was to proclaim Zebra, and his descendants, guardians of all waters in the endless grasslands.

Since then, Zebra's clan, wondrously striped in black and white, have lived mainly in the great, grassy plains of Africa, where eagle's descendants continue to fly overhead to this day.

Baboon ended up living high among the rocks, barking fiercely at every big or little thing which he saw move, for no apparent reason. Still holding his tail stiffly up to ease the stinging of his tender bald patches. He never troubled the Green Desert animals again.

From those days on, Baboon's descendants have lived mainly in the mountains, sporting bald bottoms.

The moral of this story, you say? All waters were made free for all to enjoy. And Zebra's stripes remind us of that, to this day. For you see, it was written in black and white.

CHAPTER 3

HOW GIRAFFE STRETCHED HIS NECK

Long, long, ago somewhere in Africa, when all the people and animals were new. There lived an animal called Giraffe. Do not be fooled, if you know what a Giraffe looks like now because this does not tell you how he got to look like he looks now, or what he looked like before he got to look like he looks now. Confused yet?

In those days, Giraffe would forage for food in shrubs, bushes and small trees, which grew in such abundance in ancient times. But his favourite food, of all foods, was the juicy leaves of the Tamboti tree. You may not be aware, but the Tamboti grows tall, having branches high off the ground. Nevertheless, the small trees that grow among their tall parents were and are much loved by Rhino and Kudu, but of the two, it was Kudu that most bothered Giraffe.

Kudu, Giraffe thought, was such a greedy animal with his habit of eating all his tongue could wrap around. Starting from the lowest branches on up till he left nothing for poor Giraffe who loved Tamboti above all! The competition between these two animals had become too much for good-natured Giraffe to tolerate.

So, you see, before Giraffe got his long neck, he was like his cousin Okapi. I hope you know Okapi? He lived elsewhere in deepest, darkest Africa and was not so exactly tall also. In fact, Giraffe and Kudu were about the same tall as one another, both possessing long legs and graceful necks. Although still somewhat shortish, Giraffe then was more shortish than Kudu.

But even worse than that, Kudu, with the benefit of his long and curly horns, hooked and pulled down the nice juicy bits. Thereby he made short work of the lower branches of any tree, even stripping them bare in front of Giraffe, leaving him none.

EVEN THE BEST LAID PLANS

AS USUAL, GIRAFFE WAS out foraging when it all happened, and it all happened because of one tree. The tree in question he came upon was a big, fat, tall Tamboti tree. You get big, fat and tall, you know. Giraffe, to his excitement, noticed this mighty tree growing, on the bank of a little stream.

There conveniently placed at the base was a large dead tree trunk, evidently washed down the stream by a heavy storm. This helpful trunk came to rest right under that big, fat, tall Tamboti tree, the perfect place for Giraffes scheme. Closer inspection revealed the log was indeed in the most suitable position. Giraffe then devised his master plan, in his opinion, that is. Intending to keep his next move secret, he quickly searched all around for Kudu up and down the banks of the stream. Kudu was nowhere in sight, so straight away, using the log as a step, Giraffe reached higher than ever before, each bite seeming much more delicious than the last.

Giraffe was happily eating his fill, stretching, and straining every which way. Reaching higher and higher into the tree, till enticingly close, he saw an orchid in full flower within reach. Now if there is anything to tempt Giraffe, this was it. The orchid was well placed in the fork of two branches, but forgetting he was on a log, he strained forwards.

Suddenly!

Whoosh...oopsy, bitsy, itsy, there went Giraffe, launching himself headlong straight into the crook of that tree. Well-anchored between the cleft of two branches, he hung from his neck wearing the orchid on his head with its flowers tickling his nose. Meanwhile, dislodged by Giraffe's efforts, the log slipped out from under him, rolling down the bank, into the bottom of the stream, way out of reach of his frantic feet. Of all the things to happen, for trying to eat a few leaves in peace, this had to be one of the worst.

Then, worst of all, Giraffe could feel his neck stretching as he hung there. He struggled, he strained, he pulled but try as he might, he could not break loose, for the reason that his legs and feet hung free in mid-air. How long he dangled there before Monkey found him is anyone's guess.

It was getting late, and the sun was settling to rest beyond the distant mountains. The trees were growing long shadows around Giraffe when Monkey happened by.

"Hellooo. What have we here?"

This clever, or not so clever, witticism came from Giraffe's tree-climbing simian friend. Who, having shimmied down a vine, bounded down shaking the branch where poor Giraffe helplessly hung. Musing to himself, he looked Giraffe straight in one eye.

"Is this some kind of new exercise for the neck?"

An even less smart remark.

"I say, are you comfortable hanging around like that? Did you know you could kill yourself that way?"

Never mind, Monkey's lines are definitely in need some work.

IN NEED OF HELP

FORTUNATELY, GIRAFFE through clenched teeth, managed to mumble out for Monkey to get him help.

If you think his neck was sore, think about his teeth for a moment.

"Syii sham stuuk sheerr... geet shellpp."

"I think you said geet, I mean, get help. Is that right?"

"Sheesh. Ploo, ploo, ploo."

"Oh. You want me to remove this orchid tickling your nose?

"Shanks."

"Not a bad vocabulary for an ensconced tree ornament. I'll go and get Baboon and some others. Hang tight till I return, pray no rain or termites come before I get back."

See what I mean! Swiftly he disappeared through the trees to find his cousin and some others. When Monkey returned, he brought not only Baboon but his wife, Gorilla, Chimpanzee, Elephant, Hippo, Warthog and even Python, whom he had passed along the way nearby.

Before Giraffe could say mmmfff, Elephant, Monkey, Baboon, his wife, Hippo, Gorilla, Chimpanzee and yes, even Python. In fact, the whole crew began tugging on his legs while Warthog cheered them on. First one leg, then the next, stretching all four, till they touched the ground. Suddenly Giraffe, found himself standing on his own four stilts, freed his own neck.

See? That is how Giraffe became the tallest animal of all time, with stretched everything.

Since that day of Giraffe's big stretch, he found he could reach everywhere the other animals could not, high into the trees he most wanted. And he ate orchid flowers to his heart's content, to pay them back for tickling his nose on that fateful day.

But an unusual thing had happened to Giraffe. He lost his voice. Imagine that. No voice. As a result, all giraffe are now silent creatures. But sometimes, and only rarely, they snort through their nostrils at danger.

From that day, all of Giraffe's descendants go about silently, nibbling the tender leaves of the tallest of trees, eating the delicious flowers and tastiest shoots, only they can reach!

The moral of the story, you say? Careful where you stick your neck out, things could change for you, in ways you could never guess.

CHAPTER 4

THE CHIEF, THE SUITOR AND THE KENGE

Long, long, ago somewhere in Africa, when all the people and animals were new. There was a Chief with fine daughters and numerous suitors from whom he would receive many cattle. Chiefs, along with important men in the tribe, traded their daughters to husbands in exchange for cattle. This is commonly called lobola amongst many of the peoples of Africa.

Although, there is a twist in this tale since it involves a kenge. What is a kenge, you may ask? Well, a kenge is of the African dragon family, who lives on land and in water, but makes its home in tree hollows. So, let's read on, to find out how the kenge fits into the twist of this African folktale.

Our story begins with the arrival of a young suitor to see this Chief of a certain village in Africa. He was a tall, strong, handsome young man, well clothed in fine tribal dress. From the look of him, the Chief could see he was a wealthy young man, which by his dress style, came from an elite family.

"Yes, my son, what is your name? Moreover, what do you want of me."

"My name is Addo sir. From the plain's village. I have come to ask for your daughter's hand in marriage."

The Chief roared with laughter.

"Addo my son, I have many daughters, you will have to give me the name of this daughter you seek to marry."

"My apologies sir, I am both nervous and excited. I know her as princess Thandi."

"Ah, this is a special daughter to me Addo. Also, I watch over her most jealously. You will have to have many cattle, for her price is high."

"I believe I can pay sir."

"You will be surprised at her price."

The Chief called the young man over to him, then asked him to stretch out his hands. From the look of his hands, the Chief could see he was a hard worker.

The Chief did not decline his daughters' hand in marriage. This would defeat the object for him as well as for his daughter. Instead, he told Addo to wait five days, 'go and come' on the sixth day. 'Go and come,' if you know Africa, is an ancient custom still in practice in some places today.

The young man did as he was told, going home and returning on the sixth day. Even though the excited young man arrived back at the appointed time, he was surprised at the Chief's answer.

"Go and come' tomorrow young man."

THANDI AND THE KENGE

NEXT MORNING EARLY, princess Thandi with her maidens, went to fetch water at the river as well to bathe as usual. But this time, arriving at the river, she saw a strange creature drinking on the other bank.

As soon as the creature caught sight of her with her company, it darted off, then in a loud voice, while it climbed a tree, it shouted at the girl.

"You are ugly."

She stood wide-mouthed, gazing after this creature climbing the tall tree. Thandi had never seen such a being before. Furthermore, it spoke, then worse than that, it insulted her! Also, as a Chief's daughter, she had never been spoken to in such a manner before.

"Who do you think you are? I am beautiful. Ask these maidens. Ask my father, he is the Chief."

"Ugly, ugly, I said. That old goat would not know something beautiful if it stared him straight in the face. I, of course, am beautiful."

"My father will sort you out. I am going to tell him right now."

The princess was so upset she left off bathing to hurry home, calling out to her father, as soon as she thought he was in earshot.

"Father, I have seen a beast with a long tail which ran away up a tree, shouting nasty things at me. It also insulted you, my father!"

The Chief calmed Thandi down, inviting her to sit next to him. Then he asked what the nasty beast said and what it looked like. After describing the creature, the Chief had no trouble identifying it.

"That is a kenge, my beautiful daughter. Do not let it trouble you. He has a bad mouth on him, that one. I have plans for him. Let us go, show me where it is. When I see where he is for myself, I will arrange to have him taken care of for good."

They went together, taking with them a small group of warriors in the event they saw a chance to catch the kenge. When he saw it, the Chief recognized the kenge at once. But it was up in the topmost branches, perhaps sensing the danger. It had gone where no human climber could reach it, with any kind of safety. Also, he did not want to kill it. The Chief was greatly pleased this happened because he had been looking for this kenge for some time.

ADDO'S GREAT TASK

THE CHIEF THOUGHT HOW well things were working for his plan concerning the young suitor. Making up his mind that on the young man's return, he had just the task for him.

When Addo arrived the next day, the Chief was ready for him.

"Young man, if you want to marry my daughter, you must catch a large kenge up in the top of a tree."

Addo was somewhat disconcerted when he heard this, but only asked to be shown the tree and the kenge. Escorted by two of the Chief's warriors, he was shown the huge smooth tree with the kenge still in the top branches. When Addo saw it, he was filled with hopelessness, going away mournfully.

On Addo's return to the village, the girl's father could see the young man was less than pleased with life.

"Well, where is the kenge?"

The young man looked at the Chief somewhat perplexed.

"I am stumped as to how to get that kenge out of its tree. I planned maybe to chop the tree down, but when the tree landed, it would simply run away up another tree."

"Well then, you cannot have my daughter in marriage. I told you she came at a high price. I suggest you think of a plan. When you do, you can try again."

So, Addo went back to his own village filled with heartache. When he arrived home, he found the old men sitting in the meeting place, deep in discussion. As he turned to leave, one of the ancients seeing Addo looking dejected approached him.

"Are things getting established for your wedding, Addo?"

"Much trouble over there, sir!"

"What sort of trouble is there yonder?"

The youth told his story to the old man who called him aside from the meeting.

"Go fetch a goat and a dog to take with you to where the kenge lives. Also get two vessels, one you will use for pap, the other for meat, next, get a bundle of green grass. Further, bring a bowel of organ meat, which I will prepare the way the kenge likes it, a secret from our old traditions."

Addo did as the wise man advised, who in turn, immediately went to work preparing the flesh. When he finished cooking the meat, he began constructing a sturdy net. This net was weighted around the rim, fashioned in the manner of the old hunters. When the net was completed, he proceeded to teach Addo how to use it. Well pleased with his pupil and satisfied he had done his all, the wise man placed the net in a sack, folding it in a special way, this he then hung about Addo's shoulders, to get the fit right.

Before Addo made his way back to the kenge, the wise old man explained in great detail how to go about capturing the cunning, dangerous beast. The only way the ancients had learned to catch a kenge was with much experience, like slowly, slowly catch a monkey. Calm patience, with deft and craftiness, was needed for this one. One false move and all could be lost.

"Listen well, my son. When you get there, go to the base of the kenge's tree. On the sun side of his tree, find two trees a little way off, where the kenge can see what you are doing. Tie up the goat to one tree, then the dog to the other. Place the pap and meat in front of the goat, not the dog, then place the grass in front of the dog. Go off away into the bush, like you were leaving them to eat their food. Circle round to hide somewhere on the shade side of the kenge's tree. Making sure you are well hidden from the kenge's view. Kenges always climb up and down on the shade side of trees, using the shade as camouflage. Here you will remain well hidden, till you see the kenge go around to the sun side to steal the meat from the goat because he knows goats do not eat meat."

ADDO AND THE KENGE

THE YOUTH DID AS THE old man had spoken, taking the goat and the dog with their food, he went to see the Chief. The young suitor told the Chief he was going to try again.

"You were beaten the first time, but I see this second time you are determined, so I believe you will succeed. Go, try again. I will be waiting."

Addo went once more to the tree where the kenge lived. He immediately went to work finding two suitable trees for both animals, as the wise man told him. The whole time he ignored the kenge, making as if he was not there. After he gave both animals water at the river, he tied them up as the old man had told him. He laid down the bowl of pap with the meat in front of the goat, then he gave the bundle of grass to the dog. As he left, he loudly told the two animals.

"I am off to hunt, I will return as soon as I get something. You animals eat nicely."

Picking up his bag, he headed off into the bush. Circling around out of sight, he made his way back to the shadow side of the kenge's tree as the old man instructed.

Addo was fully aware of the dangers of the kenge, from the many tales he heard growing up. It could easily break his arm with a single swipe of its tail, or bite a large piece out of his flesh with its poisonous teeth. Therefore, Addo stayed his distance till the moment was right, biding his time. Watching carefully from his hideaway, he saw the kenge come down out of his tree, heading straight for the bowl in front of the goat.

This was his chance. Quickly he pulled out his net, going back beyond the tree where the kenge went, Addo crept closer while the kenge noisily ate. Sneakily jumping up, he threw his net over him in one motion. Immediately, the kenge tried to attack him, wrapping himself up tighter and tighter. The more he struggled and wriggled, the more the net bound him. When he was well and truly knotted up, Addo using extra rope tied him even faster.

The intrepid young man took good care to see the heavy monster well secured. Because he could not carry such a large beast, he left it lying there. He ran off to tell the Chief, who sent warriors to bring it back to him. When the warriors arrived with Addo's prize, they placed it at the Chief's feet. Seeing this monster up close was more than the Chief could take. He jumped to his feet, dancing backwards and forwards around his new prize, talking to it the whole time.

"Addo, you have now become my son. You are a brave cunning young man, well capable of taking care of my daughter. For what you have done by bringing me the kenge, you may marry Thandi. 'Go and come,' bring your family and friends, in three days the wedding celebrations will be ready."

After bidding farewell to Thandi, the Chief and the warriors, Addo returned home with his dog followed by the goat, his hard work for Thandi's hand finally fulfilled. Addo's village greeted him with wondrous admiration for what he had done, making a big feast in his honour. To cheering, praises and laughter, he was made to tell his story over and over from every angle imaginable.

Three days later, accompanied by family and friends, it was a happy Addo who returned to the Chief's village to a hero's welcome.

A huge feast was laid on by the Chief, in which everyone in his village took part. While the people made merry, gifts were brought for the happy couple. All that day and into the early hours of the following morning, they partied.

The moral of the story, you say? The challenges of life are better overcome when you have people who stand by you.

CHAPTER 5

THE SAN AND THE GREAT STORM

Long, long, ago somewhere in Africa, when all the people and animals were new. One long season of drought had gripped the land - not an uncommon circumstance for Africa. Man and beast were forced to travel far and wide in their pursuit of nourishment.

This, however, was destined to dramatically change, also not too uncommon for Africa. Once again, on a normal day like most other normal days, a hunter, wait, let me digress. This was no ordinary hunter. This was none other than one of the San hunters.

If you are unfamiliar with the archetypes of the continent, let me introduce to you to the San hunter-gatherers and speakers of the !Khung and Kx'a click languages. They are a light, leathery-skinned, short, honey-coloured people well versed, no, extremely well versed, in African survival. Born from generations of knowledge concerning all things nature, from food, and medicine to the worship of one God, possessing extraordinary courage.

Unlike other tribes of this continent, they do not amass possessions, worship ancestors, own livestock, make war, or plant anything. The San simply live off the natural supply of Mother Nature as it was, as it is, and as it will be. Choosing rather to live free together, as their friends the animals did, whom they knew, loved and respected. These are a people who believe, 'To smite another human, you will harm yourself.'

Our San friend Xubi, pronounced 'tsu' while sucking inwards with the tongue on the upper palate as in 'tsubi,' went out seeking food for the little group of people camped on a small, well-positioned knoll. This knoll, surrounded by a smattering of ancient trees, and situated alongside an extinct sandy river bed, had been used by our hunter's nomadic ancestors for many generations' past.

As our hunter was making his way to the hunting grounds, he wore nothing but the traditional loincloth. Around his waist, he carried his ostrich eggshell filled with water, its drinking hole stopped up with straw and held in a purpose-made, softened animal skin bag. Over his shoulder was his treasured, much-needed bow with its essential poisoned arrows. Together with them in the quiver were his fire sticks.

This quiver, attached by thongs at the top and bottom, hung over his left shoulder behind his back. As he went, he gently poked with his digging stick at certain bulbs, to see if they were ripe for the picking. Holding his spear vertically in his left hand, he also clutched the thong to his quiver hanging over his shoulder behind him. As he walked, he looked for tsamma melons, which grow on vines along the surface of the sand.

Admiring his surroundings on this crisp, early spring morning, he listened to the birds speaking of the day's conditions in their songs. As a San man and essential to survival, he was practised in the art of hearing how the birds spoke of matters surrounding them. This was done by means of the many tunes they used from day to day and moment to moment, indicating surrounding conditions. Also, their pitch and their melody spoke of matters they observed, although to Xubi, these sounds came as words. Listening as he went, he made a note of what they were singing.

"The rain is coming, the rain is coming, the animals are far, the animals are far."

Xubi sang back to the birds as he quietly went his way.

"Thank you, my little friends, thank you, my little friends, the animals are near, the animals are near, where is the Ingududu, where is the Ingududu?"

This Ingududu is the southern ground hornbill, also known as the rainbird to the tribes from this region. It is said, till you hear the Ingududu sing, it is not going to rain. The green desert, as our name suggests, is a sandy tree-speckled grassy region enjoying little rain.

Although it was not always so. The San people believed their land was once an ancient swamp many, many, long seasons ago. This they said could be proved by the ancient river beds crisscrossing their desert.

Every few generations, there came special seasons of great abundance. The elders told of how, in this season, the region changed its entire appearance, to flourish with plants and birds, beyond all imagination. They spoke of birds flocking from distant regions of the continent, many, many, days walk away. They told of how these came to bask and feed off the plentiful food seeming to appear from nowhere, rising like a carpet from deep within the sand.

There are creatures there, they knew, that lived deep within the earth for aeons of time, waiting for this great happening. When it came, they emerged from their dormant state to live for a short but luscious season. Only to return to the depths of the earth when the waters subsided, disappearing once more to sleep till the next reawakening.

Deep in thought, pondering on these and many other ancient mysteries, Xubi wondered about the rain the birds were singing of, when just then, the Ingududu called.

THE HUNT

TRAVELLING A LONG WAY from home, Xubi had traversed two ancient river beds. The thought of rain strongly present in his mind, while hearing the constant call of the Ingududu, but still it was way off in the distance. Suddenly, another Ingududu answered, this time close by. Instantly he looked up from the fresh tracks he was following. Scanning the horizon for signs of approaching rain more carefully this time, but there were none.

Continuing in the pursuit of the family's meat, he set out beyond his regular hunting grounds still on the trail of his fresh spoor. As fortune favours the seeker, so Xubi found a small group of springbuck, which he cunningly pursued and the whole time, the rainbirds called.

Ever so slowly with the patience of a leopard, Xubi stalked, crouching forward, sometimes on all fours, moving closer and closer, till he was near enough to a buck to venture a shot. With an arrow strung in his bow at the ready, he slowly rose above the bush he was using for cover, taking aim, he painfully stretched his cramped legs. High enough to get a clear shot, he held his breath, pulling back on his bowstring, slowly, slowly, almost...

'Goowaaayyyyy,'

Was the shriek from a go' way bird perched in the tree a short distance from him. The deafening, high-pitched cry sent springbuck racing for the nearest rise, disappearing over the crest as Xubi watched in disgust.

"You ought to die, you little wretch."

Looking up at the go' way, he mockingly aimed his bow in its direction.

"Yes, I would also fly if I were you. Yes, go tell your children, my children will go hungry thanks to you."

Somewhat disappointed, he stood up straight, carefully putting the poison arrow back in its place. Chiding himself for not seeing the go' way bird in the first place. Observing his surroundings afresh, he looked to see over the treed horizon. He was surprised to see in the time he started his hunt for a buck till now, a large group of storm clouds had gathered unseen. The huge storm was fast-growing and approaching quickly, prompting Xubi to make hurried tracks for home.

Before long, the winds were blowing hard against the tall trees, rocking them from side to side. The birds had stopped their singing and the Ingududus were silent, all had found a safe place to shore up against the fast-approaching storm. This was Xubi's cue. Time was of the essence. Quickly he stepped out, setting into a fast trot, back in the direction of the knoll.

AND THE RAIN CAME

FIRST, THE RAIN FELL in multiple vertical sheets, dancing up and down, driven by the winds between heaven and earth. Bright twisted walls of water glistened in symphonies of flashing light, contrasting dramatically against a bright blue sky. Then the bands of rain began to merge into one solid force. With it, darkness descended, bringing icy cold drops stinging as they peppered the bare skin of Xubi. This was a rain that spoke of the heavens opening up in a descending torrent of water. So weighty, it would have pressed a lesser man into the ground, but not our fleet-footed San hunter.

The determination to make it home before dusk was etched in the features of the shiny-faced San man as he squinted against the raindrops to keep from falling or running into things. Without the full sun, he strained to recognise where he was, when in front of him appeared an ancient river bed, one he had crossed earlier. Remembering this fact, he was relieved, knowing he should make home before nightfall.

Stepping up his pace in familiar surroundings, he ran down the embankment onto the flat ancient river bed, dodging fast forming puddles of water. Moving with the cunning judgement of a man who had many times run down kudu and eland to their deaths for the tribe's food. Smiling to himself, he remembered how he had recently run down one of his tribe's younger hunters, to demonstrate how it was meant to be done.

Over rises and down valleys he went, like the very wind that was chasing him. Lightning shining his way over the glistening hard rain-soaked sand, with bare feet slapping the earth, his ears thudded with every step. On he went, a man against the elements to survive. Moving as fast as he could, his spirit began to soar as he ran. Dreaming the dream of the eland, his rhythm becoming one with his mighty friend. Arching his tongue, he hissed air between his clenched teeth in time to his splashing feet.

"Tjie, tjie, tjie, tjie, tjie, tjie..."

With the taste of iron from his straining, lungs, Xubi's relaxed, his cheeks shook up and down in perfect harmony with each tensing of his muscles. As he rhythmically swayed from side to side, he nodded his head, dreaming the dream of his mighty friends. Of the gemsbok straining over the hot dunes. Of the zebra in full gallop across the plains. Of the springbuck prancing in the fresh morning air. Of the cheetah in pursuit. Of the kudu weaving between the trees under and around the bushes. Of the impala as he mounted up over the brush, with horns on his back, kicking heels into the air. Free, oh, so free, ever conscious of his feet striking the sand in time with his heart.

"Go Xubi, go Xubi, go Xubi, go..."

An overcomer, victorious, majestic, in his world, united with a common will to survive and thrive.

One more sharp descent and almost home, he plunged into the waist-high surging mass of rushing water. Struggling, as he waded for the other bank, the lightning showed him the way. Not far, he could see the other bank close by.

A man not familiar with water, his rhythm slowed to sure-footed moves. Rocking from side to side, first against and then with the water, against and with the flow, with every powerful step, in a rolling action, he heaved forward.

Pain was all he felt when a heavy unseen object struck him in his left side. Down it pressed him, into the rush of water but swim he could not. In agony, he spluttered to the surface gasping for air, groping at the object that hit him. He held on with every mite of his strength, pulling himself upward and over, discovering when on top, it was an uprooted tree. Exhausted and short of breath the effort caused a coughing spasm forcing gushes of water from his lungs. Over forward, his body dropped, draping over the tree trunk. Almost conscious and in terrible pain, his hands fished for a branch to hold onto.

No sooner had he got a good grip when his tree hit an object under the water spinning them around. The sudden shock sent cold pangs of pain stabbing into Xubi's lungs like long sharp thorns up and down his left side.

This spin put the driving force of the water at his back and with that, he could see down this colossal ancient river, the lightning strikes showing him the way the torrent was driving him and his tree. But where he did not know? What he knew to be reality had left his world when the tree hit him and time no longer mattered. He hung on to consciousness, desperately hoping for a change to improve his lot. Straining to stay on and rounding many endless bends, his tree without reason suddenly washed headlong towards one bank.

Hitting a sand bar, it unceremoniously tipped him up and over his head, onto his back on a sand bar, beyond the raging sea of water. Leaving him, writhing silently as he arched his back, seeking a position that would ease the pain. The tree in the meantime left him, rushing on down the seething watery mass, to its own destiny in the desert sand. Xubi, still keeping silent in his agony, instinctively checked about for his safety. Trying to gather his thoughts, he rested up for a moment in the most comfortable position he could find. Realising he had been travelling many miles in the opposite direction to that of his home he hoped destiny had put him in a better place. Sick from the icy cold weather and the taste of blood in his mouth, he could feel water still in his lungs. Cautiously getting to his feet, with sloshing water in his stomach he felt top-heavy, so aided by his hands, he made his way up the bank toward an old tree. There he settled down to rest against the abundant stem of a mighty Marula.

Non-stop shivering, he holed up through a painful, rainy night with little rest. At first light, he reached for his ostrich shell containing his water, tied about his waist, it had slid around to his right side, still intact. Relieved, he put his hand up to his chest to feel for the thong which held his bow and arrows and with them, his fire sticks. Nothing, they were gone, as was his spear, and with it, his digging stick, swallowed by the watery deluge.

Saddened by his great loss, he again scrambled on all fours to find a useful stick with which he could defend himself. The effort caused him so much pain, he instantly cramped up into a tight ball, instinctively conscious not to utter a sound while he clutched at his chest. It appeared the tree that hit him had broken or cracked a number of ribs.

Once again straining to breathe as shallowly as he could to ease the pain, caused the phlegm to rise, then erupt, forcing out blood and water, spiking his pain to new levels. Rolling over and over in the sand, gasping for air in futile attempts to catch his breath, he felt an icy-cold shudder shooting up his face to set fire to his head. Then a hot, wet feverish sweat that mingled with the rain ran down his brow to burn his eyes. His ears rang so loud, he could hear no more but his thumping heartbeat. With blinding white flashes, still clutching his chest, his legs kicking him outstretched, he collapsed over sideways, gulps of wet air tearing into his throat. Finally, he lay still, his breath coming in short sharp, fast bursts. His burning hot brow ever-present, the white flashes now slowly fading, his senses began to settle. His eyesight returned, his thinking, slowly some form of reality was beginning to emerge once more.

After resting a moment, abandoning his search for a stick, he clawed his way back to his tree, huddling up to its abundant stem once more, hoping no lions or hyena were anywhere nearby to smell his blood on the sand, trusting the rain would soon wash it away. Still deathly cold and soaking wet, the taste of blood strong in his mouth, he took a mouthful of water from his ostrich shell to wash it out, then closing it again, he curled up to sleep. Mercifully he dozed off, awakened a short while later by the sound of lions roaring. Ignoring their roars through the night, he snatched sleep whenever his body would allow him. Eventually, Xubi made it through another rainy night.

A STRANGER ON THE SCENE

AFTER THREE DAYS, HUDDLED under the low boughs of that sumptuous tree, he waited for the sun to warm his aching limbs, but there was none. The rain continued unabated. With the inner strength given to one exercised in great suffering, he managed to rest. Of one trained to overcome hardships, there are few like the San.

On the fourth day, still solidly overcast but raining a little less, there appeared, out of nowhere a little bird, who sat in the tree close by Xubi's head, singing. Surprised by its suddenness, he looked up to see it was a honeyguide, chirruping away as it moved done closer, constantly eyeing him as it went.

"Chekit-chekit-chirr, chekit-chekit-chirr. Tchit."

In the many years of his wandering the green desert, this was the first time a honeyguide had come to him. Normally he called for the honeyguide. Taking it for the providence he hoped it to be, he chirped back at the little bird repeatedly in a high-pitched tone.

"Birrrrr yum, birrrrr cold, birrrrr cold."

"What is your name, San man. Tchit."

Shocked to hear the little bird's directness, he answered accordingly himself.

"My name is Xubi and what is yours?"

Suddenly, the little bird flew up and perched back onto the branch the way it had come. Looking back at his new friend with head half-cocked to one side, as if he was sorry for the forlorn-looking man sitting below him.

"My name is Tjikatie and I will help you get food for both of us. Yes, for both of us it is. Tchit."

"Well, Tjikatie, how are you going to do that?"

"I can see a termite nest from here. We can start there. It is a nest, is it not? A termite nest. Let us go Xubi. Tchit."

Keen to see its whereabouts, Xubi carefully stood up by sliding his bare back up the tree trunk, wriggling his shoulder blades to avoid getting scratched by the bark. Upright, he looked in the direction his little feathered friend indicated. Lo-and-behold, sure enough, there it was, a termite mound not far off. That is exactly what he needed. But how was he going to dig into it?

Putting the thought out of his mind, for the time being, Xubi set out in the direction of the mound on hands and knees. All this time Tjikatie fluttered nearby. Halfway there he knelt on a sharp object, which turned out to be a rock. What good fortune! Xubi was encouraged, things may be turning for the better after all. When he came to the anthill, he found an aardvark had raided it not long before, creating a large hollow cave toward the middle of the mound. His little feathered friend regularly uplifting his spirit with its beautiful songs as they went.

"Grubs, Xubi, it is the grubs we need. Grubs, grubs, grubs. Tchit."

Using his newly found sharp rock, careful not to erupt in another coughing spasm and using only his right hand, he began digging where the termites had repaired the old damage. Once opened, he came to the indispensable ant grubs his aardvark friend had previously feasted on.

"Come, my little friend, eat."

Eating as much as his stomach would allow, he rested against the damaged nest to absorb the little warmth created by the ant's internal combustion. Xubi was aware this heat came from the ant's fungal gardens deep within.

"Are you full Xubi? Tchit."

"Oh, yes, thanks to you. Are you?"

"I am, thank you, thank you. I will see you tomorrow, tomorrow my friend, till tomorrow. Tchit."

His happy honeyguide flitted off through the drizzling rain out of sight.

After two days in his makeshift shelter, the rain started abating, bringing cold breezes in its stead. Xubi snuggled tightly into the warmth of his anthill, then watched the termites once again repair their home next to him after his latest foray.

A brief instant before darkness fell, the setting sun showed itself for a moment through a gap in the clouds. The sight elevated Xubi's hopes for the next day. Since the rain was letting up, he needed protection from predators out on a hunt, if he was to make it safely through another night. Above him, growing up through the old anthill was a flat-top thorn tree where Tjikatie sat when visiting. Venturing out for a moment, he broke a few small branches causing himself remarkable pain, but fortunately no coughing. These branches with their thorns for protection he packed as best he could to minimise the opening to his shelter.

THEN THE SAND BEGAN TO BLOSSOM

SURE ENOUGH, EARLY the next day, through bands of red clouds the flaming morning sun, majestically mounted up over the dark tree line, the giant radiating light to a cold and sodden world. After heralding its way over the horizon for the first time in many long, wet days, the excitement filled our brave nomad's heart watching from his self-styled dugout. Xubi never wasted a moment, facing the sun to warm himself and drawing from it, all the strength it was able to give him. Beginning with weak rays, he patiently waited in hope, as it grew into an enormous yellow ball with its powerful, welcoming presence, warming him and all the world about him.

This day, with the arrival of the sun, Xubi's world erupted into a mystical, musical, paradise, with new flowers, birds and insects, as far as the eye could see. He had never in his life heard so many frogs and insects. Then it happened, up his back they went, the vibration of hundreds of termites fluttering their wings as they climbed to see the sun to fly. This is what he needed. Termite breakfast. Just not on his back. Brushing some out of his ears, he moved to help them see more of the sun. When those left his back, he turned to the nest, grabbing one after another and into his mouth they went. Flying termites are one of the San's great delicacies which come but once a year in the green desert. These little creatures are a lifeline to the weak or sick, therefore a fitting end to the winter months, with a cornucopia beginning to the summer plenty.

Birds from far and wide were drawn to feast at Xubi's anthill. As were many agamas, lizards, mongoose and meerkats great and small. And of course, Tjikatie was there, chirruping away as he feasted with the San man in attendance.

"Come San man, we must get the honey. Remember the honey, the honey? You must remember the honey? It is honey time, honey time for you and me. Tchit."

"Naturally Tjikatie, you lead the way."

The thought of honey excited Xubi beyond belief. First, there were the termite grubs, then the sun, after these the flying termites, now the honeyguide with honey. With the sun and these good foods, he should be back to health in no time.

"Check, check, chekit chirr, check, check, chekit chirr. Me and you to the honey tree, follow me, to the honey tree, the honey tree. Tchit."

"Birrrrr yum, birrrrr yum. Remember my injuries, little bird. Go slow."

He was sure the excited little creature could not possibly know how injured and weak he was. Slowly, he followed to the next tree, then no sooner had he reached it when Tjikatie flew off again, calling him to follow, flying back and forth, giving him encouragement. This went on for some time with the bird chirruping and Xubi answering as he followed. Suddenly, he was enveloped by the sound of bees, humming and flying all round about him and his little honeyguide. Observing the bird, he saw it go to a crevice, not overly high off the ground, in the hollow of a large leadwood tree. The whole time, that little hyperactive bird flew around and around with its encouraging songs.

"Come San man, this is a feast day, to feast for strength and happiness, for happiness and strength. A honey feast for sweetness and goodness, goodness is sweetness. Tchit."

"Slow down my little friend. Slow down. I must plan a plan to get the honey out."

Sitting down on the log of another ancient Leadwood tree from many generations' past, Xubi began his plan to get the honey out. Chirruping, Tjikatie came to rest on a branch close overhead. Maybe he imagined, this way, he could hear Xubi's thoughts. Who knows, perhaps he could? Assessing his condition, Xubi was not sure he was up to the task of getting to the hive right then. While observing, he noticed the size of the bees. And saw they were stingless Mopani bees, a welcome sight indeed, uplifting his spirit. These are small little bees, well known by the San to have great powers of healing. Xubi convinced this little honeyguide was providentially sent, looked up at him sitting on the branch above his head.

"My little Tjikatie, thank you for bringing me here. I am sick and I must make a home here to protect me from the dangers of the night. There is little sunlight left and I must make the best of the day. Tomorrow we will get the honey out."

"Yes, tomorrow. Tomorrow is good. Honey and sweetness for tomorrow. Tchit."

Satisfied Xubi went to work as best he could with his little friend chirping away as he worked. First, he gathered thorn branches, packing them in a circle under the tree, enclosing himself and the hive within it. This seemed to please Tjikatie greatly, perched above his friend he quietly sang to him as he worked away. When the small enclosure was complete, Xubi went off to find the Mopani saplings with the straight stems, which are impervious to insect attack. With his sharp rock, he laboured hard to sever two sticks. One long stick for extracting the honey and one short one, to act as a spear for self-protection. After a quick search, Xubi found a queen tree from which he made fire sticks. Gathering firewood on the way back, he found a dry abandoned eagle-owl's nest in the hollow of a tree, which he took for his kindling.

When Xubi arrived back to his enclosure, the sun was snuggling down below the tree line for the night. Across the great giant's red face, he watched as flock after flock of unknown kinds of birds, ones he had never seen before make their way to roost for the night. He had heard of ducks and geese, but never of the long-legged straight birds and the ones with big hanging bills. All the while, Xubi worked on his kindling and before long, a handsome fire was underway.

Munching tsuwi berries, he had collected on the way, he waited for enough coals to form for his work. When ready, he fashioned his spear and a long stick in the hot coals sharpening and stripping the bark. Life almost seemed normal with his happy little bird singing over his head as he worked. Fascinated, his little companion watched till darkness fell before chirping good night, flying up higher into the abundant Leadwood tree.

"Goodnight Xubi. Honey in the morning, honey in the morning. Tchit."

"Yes, my little friend. Honey in the morning. Goodnight."

Overhanging his fire, the majestic tree reflected the flickering flames against its huge limbs and stem, which would be visible for a far distance across the green desert. If any of the San tribes were close, they would see the light and come to his aid the next day, knowing no San man would light a fire under any tree, except to bring attention to himself. The bees were silent for the night, unaware what the morrow held in store for them.

All around Xubi insects, frogs and night noises he had never heard before, sounded in abundance, as far as he could hear. They mingled with other night sounds, like the owl, the nightjars, the tree frogs, lions, hyenas, and jackals which he knew only too well. The nights were still cool from the abundant rain, therefore, before settling in for the night, Xubi dug a small trench into which he pushed red-hot coals, covering them over with sand again to make a warm bed. Snuggling up to the fire, he lay down on his new warm bed for his crucial night's sleep. Lying comfortably on his right side facing the fire, he planned his next day's journey, thinking how wonderful it was going to be, to show his people he was still alive and be with his family once more.

Xubi never remembered falling asleep, although he was awakened to a dusky dawn by the emerald spotted wood dove's call above him, in its familiar dulcet mellow tones.

"Du, du...du; du..du..du, du..dudu, du, du, du, du, du, du, du, du, du."

Together with the emerald, a short way off, the pleasant pheasant voiced their perfectly orchestrated, high-pitch early morning greetings.

"Bitter tea leaf, bitter tea leaf, bitter tea leaf, bitter tea leaf."

Whilst announcing their praises to the day, the eastern sky was turning a paler shade of grey, promising Xubi a perfect day for travel.

ON THE HOMEWARD RUN

UP AND AT IT, HE GATHERED his previous day's supplies of thick green bark, with it, his pile of moss and his scrapings of gwei skins, from his previous night's dinner. Onto the broad piece of bark, Xubi scooped hot coals from the Leadwood branch he left to smoulder through the night. Carrying these with him, he made his way to the beehive. Needless to say, Tjikatie was excitedly flying around and around his head, chirruping non-stop.

"Check, check, chekit, chirr, check, check, chekit, chirr. Are you ready Xubi? Tchit."

"I am ready, let us go and get the honey."

Standing under the bees' nest, he raised the bark as high as possible, filling the bees' opening with smoke. The bees flew from the hive, thinking they were on fire but calmed by the smoke they flew higher. As the bees left the hive, Xubi grabbed his long digging stick. With it, he carefully pulled out bundles of honeycomb filled with honey. The little honeyguide wasted no time in feeding off the combs at Xubi's feet. The happy little lark sang away in appreciation to its gatherer as it feasted on the honey-filled wax. His friend stooped down to take some of the plenty he had gathered for the little honeyguide and himself. Indulging in their early morning bounty, they ate together.

Leaving the majority of the honeycombs intact for the bees in their hive, Xubi found a good stout, short, digging stick under the big tree. He dug a long ditch beneath the big Leadwood log to hide his long, honey digging stick. The little bird watching him the whole time.

"Little one, this is proof I will be back to use this same stick to fetch you more honey when the season is good."

"On that day Xubi, call me, birrrrr yum, birrrrr yum and I will come flying and I will come quickly. Tchit."

Revitalised by his early morning honey fest, Xubi made final preparations for the trip home. Onto his piece of green bark, he loaded enough honey-filled wax combs he felt he could easily carry. Returning to his enclosure, he transferred the honeycombs into the little basket he had woven the night before from the bark strips. Ready to go, he picked up his makeshift spear and new digging stick, waving to his little feathered friend, still gorging on his pile of honey.

"Farewell my little saviour, I will be back to see you when we can share of the bee's abundance once more. Rebuild little bees, may Mother Nature be kind to you for sharing your treasure with us."

"Go well, go swift, San man. Take care, till next, we eat sweetness together. Tchit."

First, after covering his fire with hand scoops of sand, Xubi faced the giant yellow ball forming in the morning sky.

"My great friend in the sky, guide me and give me warmth, but do not burn me this long day."

Xubi waved to the honeyguide feasting on his honey. The little bird momentarily came over, chirruping its goodbye, as his friend trotted down into the ancient river. After first filling his ostrich water shell, Xubi, heading for home wading through the gentle flowing thigh-high water.

Horizon to horizon, birds swam on the surface of the water and others with long necks like a giraffe with curved beaks, searched in the water for food. Still, there were others, filling big bills with food washed down from a great distance away, from whence the water came. Butterflies, dragonflies and many more, he knew not what they were, swarmed here and there from bank to bank. On either side, in front and behind him, he passed them on his way to the opposite bank.

After climbing the embankment, Xubi took a mouthful of honey and finally on his way, he immediately stepped out into a fast trot. As he went, he kept a sharp lookout for any predators he might run into.

At midday, he slowed down to cool his lungs now burning from the heat. Familiarity with the region where he found himself, filled him with added strength to push on, knowing he was not far from home. It was then that a troubling thought came to him. Remembering what he and the other hunters agreed before he left for his hunt that fateful day. He remembered one of the elders saying.

"Xubi if you fail on this hunt, we will have to move to the plains for this summer. It is there most of the animals have gone for food and water."

"I agree. This we will do if I come back without a buck."

It is customary for the San to follow the herds and move camp from season to season, never staying in any one camp for too long. The conversation they had was playing on his mind. Would he find anyone in camp? Putting the thought out of his mind, he ran on, making good progress even for one without damaged ribs. At the hour before sunset, when it is the custom for the animals to go for water, Xubi slowed to a walk for the first time that day.

He was home, the hunter in him paused, standing still and looking around, he held his breath and listened. Hearing children's laughter in the distance, he relaxed.

Slowly this graceful figure, profoundly grateful to be alive, quietly made his way to his family. The excitement is too hard to describe, but there was not a dry eye in anyone there till the sun went down that day.

His people had come out for him, feeding his wife and two sons anything they could not gather for themselves.

For the remainder of summer, the entire tribe feasted and marvelled at their Creator, enjoying the bountiful abundance the great storm had brought.

So, this story was added to the mighty mysteries which surround us and remembered by many, many, generations, till this time of the new beginning.

The moral of the story, you say? Never give up, always keep alert and cheerful; you never know where your next meal may come from.

CHAPTER 6

HOW ELEPHANT AND WARTHOG GOT THEIR TUSKS

Long, long, ago somewhere in Africa, when all the people and animals were new. Elephant, you may not know, was related to Warthog since forever. Although they were created decidedly different, they are cousins. It may surprise you to know, they fed on the same food. Well, almost the same food, namely roots, bark and leaves.

Of course, Warthog eats scrub, shrub and grass leaves, Elephant eats grass, bark, roots and tree leaves. Elephant drinks lots of water, making his food into tree leaf tea. I am sure you must have heard of tea? To get on with the story, pour a cup of tea or coffee, then join Elephant and Warthog as they have a life-changing experience.

Elephant, you probably did not know, could not get to eat the bark or roots of trees long, long ago. But because of Warthog, he is able to eat them now. Sound strange? Read on and see why.

ELEPHANT SEEKS OUT WARTHOG

EVEN THOUGH ELEPHANT and Warthog are family, they have always been closest friends anyway. The reason for this is, Warthog and Elephant were cousins! Yes well, that meant they were family.

You might not believe me, but Warthog and Elephant are related. Naturally, I am sure you can see why, their skin, their hair, as well as of course their tusks, especially, their tusks. On a hot bushveld day, Warthog was munching some bark and roots of a tree a storm had blown down when Elephant happened to wander by. He ambled by Warthog often. This time he stood there watching Warthog using his tusks to loosen and eat the bark and roots. Observing these actions of Warthog closely, Elephant was persuaded to quietly approach him. Warthog, of course, was not one who liked to be bothered too often. It made him too grumpy for his already grumpy old self to appreciate the company because he was already grumpy in any case. But he always tried to be polite. Because it was what was expected.

"Warthog, I love bark and roots. Can I eat some bark and roots alongside you?"

"Certainly, you can, but please be careful where you step. Last time we ate together, you nearly trod on me."

Poor Warthog, try as he may, he always sounded grumpy, on account of his nature you see. Elephant, as you can imagine, was most embarrassed with himself. But this did not stop him asking Warthog an even bigger favour. In fact, a life-changing one indeed. Something he had been dreaming about for an awfully long time. Although never getting up the courage to make a clean breast of it. But this time he was determined.

You may not know, but Warthog had huge tusks while Elephant had small tusks. For this reason, Elephant could not get to the bark and roots of the big trees. And it was for this precise reason Elephant could not keep his eyes off of Warthog as he ate.

Warthog, you see, lived under the trees, in the rain and hot sun. He many times wanted to go underground to stay out of the rain and the sun. This, I suppose could account for his grumpy nature, then also his fondness for mud. His best friend Aardvark was always inviting Warthog to stay next door, in a hole he had dug in a dormant anthill. But Warthog's tusks were far too large to get down the hole. So, he continuously went in backwards, but his head stuck out. As a result, when it rained Warthog's head got soaking wet, then badly baked in the hot sun.

That day, as it so happened, Elephant was hoping his dreams would come true, hoping Warthog would trade tusks. Since they were related, being cousins and all, he was sure they would fit. With a little adaptation naturally, but fit they would. This Elephant told Warthog.

"Warthog, we are cousins as you know"

Watching Elephant as he stared wide-eyed at him, Warthog became terribly suspicious, also noticing how his cousin was unable to hide his excitement.

"Yes."

"Well, I have an idea."

This really made all of Warthogs hair stand on end.

"Yes, I'm listening,"

Elephant deciding not to waste any more time in asking Warthog. Blurting it out.

"Can we trade tusks?"

Warthog swallowed hard, jumping up looking cross-eyed at Elephant, who at this point, lay down, even more, wide-eyed than before, eagerly hopefully, grinning and wagging his tail. Well, it's been a long time, maybe not wagging his tail. Anyway, this time Warthog swallowed even harder. But elephant insisted.

"They will fit you know because we are cousins."

Elephant, ever so hopeful Warthog would see it his way. Because in his mind it also made perfect sense not to refuse.

"Why do you want my tusks? They are hard to handle and each time I jerk my head up, they make my eyes go cross-eyed and I can't even go down a hole with them."

"Exactly, I do not need to go down holes, I need to push down trees, as well as get bark and roots with them. So, I need big tusks, just like yours. While you Warthog, need smaller tusks, just like mine, so you can go down holes."

AARDVARK SAVES THE DAY

IT WAS RIGHT THEN, Aardvark wandered by, hearing the last part of the conversation. He could not resist remarking to Warthog, his closest friend. Aardvark and Warthog have always been the bestest of friends since forever, till now.

"I would take them if I was you. Then you can go down the holes I have made for you to keep out of the hot sun and rain."

Warthog, knowing his good friend would give him wise counsel, was ever so pleased to have him come by at that exact moment. With no more time wasted, Warthog immediately traded tusks with Elephant. As you can tell. Some fitting and adjusting was necessary, but in the end, it was proven Elephant was right. Indeed, they fitted. Elephant went away as happy as a lark, whistling to himself while swinging his trunk from side to side as he went. Well, maybe not whistling, but blowing something.

So, there you have it! That is why Elephant can eat the bark and roots from the trees he has pushed down. All due to his handsome tusks he inherited from Warthog.

Even after Warthog got his new tusks that fit down the hole perfectly well, he still went down it backwards. Now poor old Warthog had some major adjusting to do. But try as he may, he could not change a habit of a lifetime. Well, it was on account of his big old tusks, which never fit down any holes. So, he settled on going down his hole backwards, as you will see all Warthog's descendants still go down holes backwards to this day.

Being well informed, you can have no doubt as to the story of Elephant and Warthog and why they have lived happily ever after, each with their own new tusks.

The moral of the story, you say? You may not know all there is to know, even about yourself. So always be prepared to listen to another's opinion, of what they think of you. Others may see you better than you see yourself.

CHAPTER 7

BLINDMAN AND HUNCHBACK

Long, long, ago somewhere in Africa, when all the people and animals were new. The region of our story has to do with two lions, a Chiefdom, two princesses, a blind man and his hunchback friend. This country in Africa where they lived, was highly fertile and productive, rain being mostly plentiful, perhaps sub-tropical, or thereabouts.

Our two heroes had grown up together because tradition in Africa dictates, someone must be appointed to look after a blind man for life. And this is usually done by friending a handicapped person to a blind person, ensuring productivity in the tribe. The hunchback, therefore, became the eyes of the blind man, elected as such by the elders of the tribe. The blind man was both intelligent and crafty, good with his hands, aided by a strong deminer, possessing a quick wit and great courage. The hunchback in his turn was likewise skilled with his hands. Yet, above all accolades, he was faithful in the execution of his nominated duty toward his blind friend. Even though they had many differences, they became inseparable and were known to their people simply as Blindman and Hunchback.

The two became well known in their region and were generous and helpful to anyone in times of need. Only requiring one another's gifts and skills to survive without the want for charity, so the men became lifelong friends. Winning the peoples respect, meant they were never short of work, ensuring boredom was not one of their misfortunes in life.

Even though they were good friends, they quarrelled an awful lot, a matter more amusing than not, since they always ended up accomplishing their tasks successfully. The one who argued the most was Hunchback. As you will see, his mischievous ways often pushed fortune in favour of wisdom. Here, Blindman had an abundance of patience, mixed with quirky craftiness, which he regularly demonstrated, proving quiet diplomacy paid off the best.

PUTTING IT ALL TOGETHER

ONE DAY BLINDMAN, IN good old African style communication, received a drum message from their local drummer. The dispatch came from a Chief of a vast region far away. This region incorporated the village where Blindman had grown up. Born to become an orphan, the Chief became his friend, mentoring him till he became of age.

On this occasion, the Chief's whole region was in a dreadful crisis involving two marauding lions. In the dispatch, he was asking for help from anyone wise and brave enough to rid them of this curse. Offering a handsome reward to anyone able to rid his kingdom of their problem.

It was from there that Blindman was sent away, to join Hunchback, in the faraway land he now lived in. Hunchback was the one chosen to look out for Blindman till death or dismissal, a role only the Chief possessed.

The drummer's recent news troubled Blindman. He pondered his old village's plight for some time, wondering if he could help and if so, how? All night Blindman hardly slept a wink. And in his wakefulness, his thoughts drifted back to his youth, thinking about those who had helped him. Were they even still alive? Believing, surely the Chief would remember him. After all, it was he who had taught him the most, like how to fish. Those memories came back to him as if it were yesterday.

"My son, I know you cannot hunt, but you need a skill to be able to eat. Come, since a blind man sees with his fingers and ears, I am going to teach you how to fish, fish well that is."

Down to the river they went, the Chief leading the way, net and club in hand. At the river they went up a tall group of rocks high up on the bank, overlooking the river.

"Remember son, always find tall rocks to climb onto when you go fishing. The crocodiles are plenty and you will not be able to see or escape them if you are on their level. Therefore, stay out of reach on high rocks like these.

Here from this lofty vantage point, the Chief first taught him all he needed to know about fishing nets.

"Feel here, my boy. This is a net. Run your hands around the knots and squares. Feel around the edge at these weights. They are made from leopard seashells filled with mortar to give weight. These weights are needed to throw far across the water and sink fast to capture the fish inside your net. You are stronger than the average young man, which is good for fishing with a throwing net."

With patience and caution, the Chief showed him how to hold the net, how to cast and what to listen out for, before casting.

"Listen with care to all the sounds. What do you hear?"

"Father, I hear birds singing, splashing water and cracking sounds from heavy horns colliding, which I know are kudu play sparring."

"Do you hear water plopping?"

"Yes, I hear a shish, then a plop."

"Those are the fish jumping out the water to feed on insects. It is them you will throw your net on, immediately after you hear that sound. There is another sound you must not throw your net over, which is a loud splash followed by a second splash. That is a crocodile catching those fish. Remember the sound."

Long hours were spent at the river with and without the Chief, till Blindman became a highly skilled fisherman. So good, the villages knew him to be the best net fisherman in all their district. Later, when he joined up with Hunchback, who also loved fishing, they often went to the big river not far from them to fish.

It was while he dwelled on these childhood memories when he hatched his plan to save the villagers from their plight. It would mean a long journey, obviously taking Hunchback along as his eyes. They would of necessity have to collect things needed along the way for his plan to work and this was another way where Hunchback was invaluable.

Early next morning, having made the decision to go, he gathered his fishing net, two tusks he had received as payment from a traveller he helped. One from a young elephant and the other a handsome large warthog tusk. Warthog were unknown in the land he had come from.

When he woke, the first thing he did was to tell Hunchback, of the long journey they were taking to a far country and for him to get supplies and make ready to travel.

Hunchback, being his custom, instantly refused to go till he knew why he should. Thinking to himself, Blindman regularly took him for granted, never asking, but always telling. This time, he was going to find out all there was to this story and in detail too. Noting Hunchback's disagreeable attitude, Blindman declared he would get someone else to share his riches.

"What riches, where?"

The shrewd and cautious Blindman seeing Hunchbacks attitude was not ready to share his news that easily, what if he, Hunchback, decided on other plans. This mission was far too important to have it go wrong at this stage.

"If I tell you, how do I know you will not leave me and go there yourself, once you know the whereabouts of the treasure?"

"If this is a treasure hunt? I will come with you."

"And?"

"And what?"

"And only if you get the supplies we must have and promise to be a faithful companion on the whole journey, helping collect necessary things along the way."

"All right, I will get the supplies. But first, how far is it?"

"Not so fast, what happened to promising to be a faithful companion till we return?"

"Yes, I promise to keep you company till we return,"

Blindman was still not fully satisfied, needing a better commitment from his friend than that.

"And help me collect the things I want along our way?"

"Now—you, 'not so fast', do you think I am your slave, to follow all your commands at the snap of your finger?"

These two knew one another far too well, for either one to be hoodwinked by the other and Blindman after their many years together, was well versed in how far he could push his friend. As you can see, Hunchback continuously tried to outwit his friend, whom he had learned was smarter than himself. This, he refused to admit, although regularly doing his best to corner Blindman, always hoping to get a better deal for himself. But Blindman was usually one step ahead of his long-time friend.

"Well, do you want the riches or not?"

"Alright, alright, let's agree to this—, I have the right to disagree till you explain why I should obey."

Shaking his head, Blindman knew what his sneaky friend was trying to do, although he went along with him, for the moment, that is.

"All right, if you agree to go along, I will answer all your questions, but only if the request is reasonable."

Receiving his friend's confirmation, Hunchback boldly added.

"Better, I will get the supplies when you tell me why and where we are going since I have given you my word."

Blindman knew if he told Hunchback the whole story, he would be too scared to go, so he doctored it a little.

"There is a village in need of help and I know the Chief well from my childhood. Remember, when you and I first met, it was from there, I had come. This Chief sent a drum message yesterday for anyone who could help. I decided to help because I know you could also do with a share of the reward offered, which is why I asked you to join me. I hope that satisfies your curiosity?"

Hunchback slowly nodded his head, realising it would be hopeless to insist on a better answer, even though he knew his friend was holding things back. After all, he asked where they were going and not why. Blindman, he felt had told him what he needed to know in any case.

"Oh, and bring a large sack on a pole."

"What for?"

"Starting already! It is for securing the treasure we must bring back. I told you we must collect necessary things on our way."

Over the next few hours, they made together their equipment and supplies needed. Filling their water skins, they left on their long journey - Blindman with a backpack and the large sack on a pole over his shoulder. Hunchback carrying the other supplies on his back, as he put it 'like a donkey,' bow and arrows hanging at his side, with spear and club in hand, for protection, they left.

THE LONG JOURNEY

HUNCHBACK LEADING THE way had become unusually quiet concerning things he saw along the way. After the close of the first day's journeying, Blindman suspected his friend was keeping back information. The next day early, before continuing their journey, he confronted Hunchback on the matter.

"There are many strange things we may have to collect along the way. Things which might be of use to us for getting and securing the treasure, these I will carry."

Hunchback, hearing the treasure might depend on his finding things and knowing Blindman would carry them, changed his mind. A little while later, he saw a dead eagle in the pathway and told his friend.

"Ah, there is a dead eagle in the path ahead."

"It is of no use to us."

This pleased Hunchback, finding on closer inspection it smelt bad. Many things were seen and reported over the next few days, but not required. Till Hunchback reported a small tortoise shell a little way off the path;

"We will need that. Gather it up; they do not have tortoises where we are going."

Giving it to Blindman, to put it in his sack. For some days, nothing of use was found, till they came upon a dead porcupine, and Blindman asked his friend to pick up one long and thick quill.

"For my plan, I can use a porcupine quill. They do not have those where we are going."

Satisfied Hunchback handed a nice long, thick quill to his friend, who promptly put it in his sack. Suddenly, there was an ear-splitting scream, mingled with load roaring, bringing deathly silence all round, not a single bird chirped, then another thunderous roar. Whatever the creature was, it roared a far fiercer almost deafening roar this time. At the same time, the ground shook from heavy thudding like an elephant storming their way. Blindman was rooted to the spot, hearing nothing from his friend, he remained fixed where he was, not knowing what to do.

"What has happened?"

"I cannot see, the sound is coming from a small valley here next to us."

Again, there was a roar and this time the trumpeting sound of an elephant.

"What's happening? Are you there? Hunchback?"

"An elephant is coming straight for us. Quickly run"

"Which way must I run?"

Hunchback's voice faded away. No answer from his friend. Blindman made the only choice he had. To remain standing right where he was, till his friend told him what to do. Just then, another big roar, followed by a big crashing sound, which shook the ground like thunder.

"Hunchback, where are you? Can you please tell me what is going on? Remember, it is you who is supposed to be my eyes. Hunchback, where are you?"

Without warning, there came a voice from right behind him.

"I'm right here, next to you."

"Oh, so you call behind me, 'next to you' now?"

"Look Blindman, I am your eyes, not your bodyguard."

"So, it's like that then. Can your eyes and mouth please let me know what has happened? What was the roar, what was the crash and what was the huge thud right next to me?"

"So many questions, which one do you want me to start with first?"

"Seeing you are so calm and confident, I think you can start anywhere you like."

"It was a hunter and an elephant."

Hunchback stood there, one eye on his blind friend, while he peered over the rise to see into the valley below, trying to get a better view of what he had run away from.

"Well... and...?"

"That was it. An elephant and a hunter."

Hunchback was still straining and searching the valley for better clues.

"And, have you suddenly become a mute in the meantime? What else, if you don't mind? Try answering my other questions. One by one."

Blindman suddenly realised the scene must have frightened his friend almost out of his wits. Remembering, it was an elephant charge which was responsible for him becoming a hunchback when he was dropped by his mother in her hurried escape. Quietly, he asked Hunchback to sit next to him, as he himself sat down in the sand. When Hunchback sat down, Blindman quietly asked him again, this time in sequence.

"Without reminding you I am blind, I need you to tell me what you saw? First, there was a loud roar. What was that?"

"I do not know, because, like you, I was also blinded, unable to see over the edge of the valley from here. Then I saw this huge animal as it came over a rise charging towards us. I think it was charging after what looked to me like a hunter, but it fell down and I lost sight of it, in front of us."

"You mean, while you were standing right behind me; all the things happened in front of me, remember. Never mind, I think you should take me into the valley, so you can have a look for me, maybe the hunter could use our help?"

Hunchback, much against his better judgment, agreed and led Blindman down into the valley where an elephant lay dead on its side, a bag lying on the ground at his head. All this, Hunchback told Blindman as they went.

"Where is the hunter then?"

"I do not know? I think he has run away or the huge animal fell on him, a bag is lying here next to a big tree."

Slowly calming down, Hunchback was gradually coming back to his senses. Blindman saw his chance to leave the scene of the crime, so as to say. Before they left, they both shouted for the hunter but no answer.

"It seems we can't do anything more here, let us be on our way, we are running late, this matter has slowed us down. But first, pick up the bag for me to carry."

It took some effort convincing his companion to gather up the bag, but when he did, they resumed their journey.

THE PRINCESSES AND THE LIONS

THE GATHERING DUSK was forcing them to seek a safe place to spend the night somewhere close by. Hunchback on his own, climbed higher, searching through the twilight, he saw some smoke coming from a hut, toward the top of a neighbouring hill.

Darkness had enveloped the weary travellers when they finally came within reach of the hut. Moving closer, they heard the sound of woman weeping inside. Blindman called to those in the hut, asking for shelter from the dangers of the night, it was a woman's voice which replied.

"Who are you?"

"We are travellers in search of shelter from the predators of the night."

"You cannot sleep here our father has built this hut for the two of us to be sacrificed to the lions. They are coming tonight to eat us."

The men were shocked to hear such a story and asked why this thing should be done? The women then told the men about the two rouge lions attacking the people and eating the villager's animals throughout the Chiefs kingdom. They also explained, they were the Chief's own daughters, who offered themselves to be sacrificed to the lions. Blindman thinking they were speaking concerning his friend's village, was even the more shocked to hear such news.

"Why are you being sacrificed?"

"The lions sent a message to the Chief, our father, via our Wiseman. Saying, they would move on to another district, if he sacrificed his two princesses on this hill."

"What is the Chief's name?"

"Chief Moolakwa."

When Blindman heard the Chief's name, he knew these were the daughters of his old friend, who had called for help using the drum messages.

"Hunchback, your capable navigation has brought us to the right place. And it appears at the right time too."

Blindman increased his persistence, exhorting the princesses to let them in. The young ladies continued to argue, insisting the Chief would be more than a little angry for needlessly endangering the other citizens' lives. They begged the men to leave, so they could be sacrificed for the sake of the whole district. After much deliberating the two men convinced the princesses, who finally let them in.

"This is where we have to stay this night. I intend to take care of the lions my way. What are your names?"

When the young woman saw the man, who did the most talking was blind, they were the more puzzled, but Hunchback assured them he knew what he was doing. Relaxing a little, the young ladies became more sociable, answering Blindman's question.

"I am the older and my father named me Chinda and my younger sister was named Mindi. And may we ask your names?"

"By our custom, I have been known as Blindman since I came of age and Hunchback, has always been my friend's name from childhood."

While they were talking, a lion, a short way from their door, roared out his demands in a booming voice.

"Who is talking in the hut? Have you come to trap us? We have come to eat our woman sacrifices, where are they? Whoever you are, you better leave before you get eaten along with the others."

The Blindman was not impressed or afraid of these marauding man-eaters. In fact, he was angry at their brash arrogance. Blinman had smelt lamp oil burning when he entered the hut. Before he addressed the lions, he asked Chinda to extinguish any lamps that were lit. This done, he opened the door a crack.

"You don't scare me, I am too big for you. My friend and I come from the land of giants. We are here to make sure you two lions behave according to what was agreed with the Wiseman to see justice done."

"What justice are you talking about? And who will make us do this justice?"

"As I have told you. We are of the giants and our lions are five times your size and it is them who will take care of you if you do not obey what I say."

"Say? Say what?"

"Are you hard of hearing? You will agree to keep your word to the Chief. You will not get his daughters as a sacrifice till you do."

"What makes you think we will listen to you. We do as we please."

"If you do not do as we say, our lions will come and kill you both."

"What is it we must agree to?"

"You must stand alongside one another and vow out aloud. We have agreed with the Chief to leave his region and not trouble it again if we receive his daughters as a sacrifice."

"How do we know you are telling the truth. We will only agree if you show us proof you come from the land of giants, as you have claimed."

Blindman fetched his bag, taking out the small tortious shell.

"This is a dead tick from one of our lions."

Throwing it out the door in the direction of the lion's voice. The lions jumped back in amazement to see such a giant tick.

"You think you're so big and tough? That does not impress a lion, we kill buffalo. The bigger you are, the more there is for us to eat. Show us more proof."

Blindman once more reached into his bag and pulled out the porcupine quill throwing it out the door right in front of the lions once more.

"That is a whisker from one of our lions."

Lions being what lions are, he would not allow himself to be intimidated, reacting in such a booming voice, his roar shook the ground and the hut. The girls who were huddled in a corner fainted from dread, but Blindman and Hunchback kept their wits about them. Once the lion had regathered his composure, he once again called out.

"I am not afraid of you. I am coming in to eat both you and the girls. When you see my teeth, you will not be so brave anymore."

"Not so fast. Do you think you have teeth the size of our lions?"

Blindman, reacting quickly, took the elephant tusk from Hunchback, throwing it out in the lion's direction. When this tusk landed in front of the pair of lions, it really made them jump back in terror. Blindman knew this by the lion's huge roar of surprise, which once more shook the ground so hard, it seemed the little hut would fall apart.

"Eish! Truly this creature has awful teeth!"

"That is not all. Here is one of the lion's claws."

Reaching into his bag once more, he threw out the warthog tusk.

"Alright, we will make the vow."

Blindman had been waiting for this moment to come. During the time this was happening, he had cleverly laid out the heavy fishing net, ready to throw.

"Stand side by side, and say these words after me-. We have agreed with the Chief to leave his region."

The lions standing side by side repeated.

"We have agreed with the Chief to leave his region."

Bindman continued his prompts.

"And not trouble it again, if we receive his daughters as a sacrifice."

No sooner had the lions begun to complete their vow, Hunchback pulled the door open. This allowed Blindman with power, deft and great accuracy to throw his net over both lions, pulling the slip cord tight in one motion.

"Quick Hunchback, light a lamp and bring the heavy animal net. Here, hand me the hammer and pegs."

Both men moved swiftly, pulling the big net over the lions, pegging it fast to the ground, while they struggled to free themselves from the strong fishing net. The extra precaution Blindman devised was undoubtedly necessary when Hunchback saw how strong and determined the lions were.

Blindman went over and hugged his friend, both sinking to the ground. There they sat for some time, silently listening to the night sounds while the lions tried in vain to chew through the tough ropes. Hunchback gazed up into the star-filled sky, thankful for having such a special friend.

THE CHIEF'S KINGDOM

HAPPY THE LIONS WERE secure the men made it back into the hut. Blindman then set to work reviving the would-be victims.

"Come my princesses you are free."

"And the lions?"

"The lions are secure. You can come and see them. We have covered them with a strong net Hunchback brought here on his back."

Hunchback holding the torch-wood lamp took the princesses out. Timidly and cautiously they went, to discover both lions well netted down for the night.

At daybreak, the thankful girls dragged both rescuers to their father's village far down in the valley. When the Chief saw them, he threw his arms into the air, raging at his daughters for abandoning their post, endangering the whole district. But the girls soon placated their father.

"Father, these men have trapped those wild beasts. They are in a big net. Send your warriors to kill them."

The Chief was incredulous, but they swore most solemnly, it was so. While he hugged his daughters as ones who had come back from the dead, they excitedly, explained to their father who the blind man was. To Moolakwa's great delight, he embraced Blindman, as he would a long-lost son. Round and round, he danced, holding onto Bindman's hands as he went. Shouting to the gathering villagers, telling them this blind man was one he knew from his childhood. As things calmed down, Blindman told the Chief about the drum message, Hunchback and how they found the princesses. How he trapped the lions in a fishing net.

"Oh, my son, you have done valiantly. Beyond what I could ever have dreamed that day I first took you fishing. How proud you have made me. You saved my beautiful daughters and brought them back to life for me."

Tears running down the Chief's face, he turned away to compose himself. Quietly he walked to his throne. Fetching his own spear, he summoned six of the bravest and strongest young warriors to kill the lions. Giving the eldest his spear.

"Young man, strike the mortal blow to both lions with this."

They soon returned bringing with them the two lion's tails they had cut off to show the Chief and the villagers. The trophies in his raised hand, Chief Moolakwa addressed his people.

"As to these men who trapped the lions and saved my daughters, what do you say I should do for them?"

The villagers replied with one accord, they ought to have his daughters as wives. The Chief turning to the four standing by his side, asked what they saw fit for their lives. The four were in one agreement, providence had brought them together and wed they must. Without wasting a moment, the Chief set forth to bring the great event to pass.

On the full moon, when the marriage day arrived, a happy father, gave away his princesses Chinda and Mindi to be wed to Blindman and Hunchback. Then his proud heart spoke out.

"Some people come to marry the perfect person. Some marry who see the perfect person in that which is imperfect. This is a day like that my people."

There followed grand celebrations throughout Chief Moolakwa's kingdom. Being free from the plundering lions, the marriage of the Chiefs two daughters, the addition of two sons, the circumstances that brought it all about, was the reason they celebrated. The festivities and feasts beginning from the Chiefs royal settlement, moved out from village to village, throughout his kingdom, lasting from one full moon to the next. These were days like non-before them had ever been.

When the celebrations came to an end, Chief Moolakwa invited the wedding couples to his royal complex. Showing them his plans for building their homes, next to his, in the place of honour.

One day, musing to himself over all the recent events which had so suddenly enveloped his life, Moolakwa thought it time to give his new sons their reward for killing the lions. Being unfamiliar with Hunchbacks character, he decided to put the man's metal to the test. To that effect, he deliberately handed him a leather pouch containing five extra-large gold nuggets, for him and Blindman to be rewarded as he saw fit.

Later, when the newly-weds were out walking along the bank of a deep gulch, where huge trees grew above a small stream. There they stopped to rest and sat down on the cool sand under a large shady jackalberry tree.

"Hunchback, let us see what the Chief has given us."

Hunchback, looking into the leather pouch, reached in and took out two gold nuggets, handing them to Blindman, then quickly closing it up again, he put it back in his money pocket. Suspecting Hunchback, for not pouring out the contents before them and knowing his inherent greed for wealth, Blindman decided to quiz his friend accordingly.

"Do I need to go and ask the Chief how many nuggets he gave you, or not?"

Hunchback was so incensed at Blindman's suggestion, he jumped up. Striking out with his walking stick, connecting his friend squarely on the back of his head, knocking him over the ledge and into the gulch. Even though his blind friend had landed awkwardly head-first into the stream below, he still jumped down after him. Landing squarely onto his own back with a heavy thudding splash himself, followed by falling rocks and debris. Angered by Hunchbacks temper, Blindman sprang up, grabbing his stick, which he saw a little way off on the edge of the stream. Startled by his own actions, he stopped short in his tracks. Turning around, he saw his attacker standing there dripping sopping wet, as straight and upright as an arrow, in the middle of the stream.

"You are no longer a hunchback and I am no longer blind. What miracle has happened this day?"

The princesses were laughing, running about clapping their hands, shouting to all those they could see, letting them know what had happened. In no time, the small ravine was flooded with mothers, fathers and scores of children, come to see the miracle. For no doubt, a great wonder had just occurred.

When the warriors from the village heard what had happened, they rushed to the little stream. Hauling up both Blindman and Hunchback, they carried them high on their shoulders, parading them throughout the village. The people following the procession were dancing, shouting and singing songs of the heroes as they made their way up to the Chief's court. There the warriors lowered the two men to the multitude's jubilation, who threw gold, silver and copper jewellery, at their feet.

These recent happy circumstances gave the men a profound change of outlook on life. Hunchback, without wasting a moment, reached into his money pouch, giving his friend another gold nugget.

"Sorry, I tried to cheat you, there were five. That was terribly wrong of me, the people know it was due mainly to you these wonderful things have happened. I would be honoured if you would count out the gifts and divide them between us as you see fit. So please, forgive me for my great wrong and thank you for your friendship, which means more to me than a dear brother, especially since you have become free to go where you please."

"I could never hold any wrong you have done me, after all the years you have been my eyes and faithful companion. Consider yourself not only forgiven, but blessed for those years you sacrificed for me. I would rather you count out the loot and take half my share as a gift from me."

As a result of their strange miracles, the two men decided not to build next to the Chief. But rather to return to their own land with their princesses. Consulting with their father-inlaw, it was agreed.

The Chief from his side sent them on their way with great wealth and his warriors as escorts.

As they were nearing the edge of an escarpment, after travelling many days, Hunchback leading the way, turned to show his friend the vast wide-open valley that stretched before them. So expansive, the mountains on the other side were obscured by the heatwave which rose from the forest floor.

"We are home, this is where we live."

Blindman seeing his homeland for the first time and deeply moved with compassion, sat down on a boulder with Chinda at his side, staring into the vast blue yonder. From afar, they heard the echoes of drums and musical choruses, laughter and the singing of praises. If our heroes thought they would escape another celebration, they were wrong. The message drummers had been hard at work. Their own people were ready for them and that night they partied.

Early on the day following after the warriors had left for home, all able-bodied men and women from the village came together where the four newlyweds were staying. The purpose? To build their new abodes. This was the way of these people and the way in which they welcomed all brides to their community.

The moral of the story, you say? Never tire of doing good, whether blind or cripple, you never know when or how your reward may come.

CHAPTER 8

SNAKE AND THE YOUNG MAN

Long, long, ago somewhere in Africa, when all the people and animals were new. A certain young man walking down a pathway came upon a tail swishing in the air from under a large rock. Stopping by it, he watched. As he watched, he realised the creature belonging to the tail appeared to be pinned to the ground beneath the rock.

Cautiously, after closer inspection, he surmised the rock must have fallen on the unfortunate animal from the pinnacle above, thereby pinning it to the ground. For a time, while observing the situation, the tail became motionless. Not meaning to be cruel, but wanting to see if the creature was dead or alive, he delicately pulled the tail. The tail jerked back, with the sound of a muffled cry coming from under the large rock.

WHY NO THANK YOU?

CONSIDERING IN HIS estimations the thing to be alive, the young man proceeded to carefully roll the rock from off the poor creature's head. No sooner was the creature's head freed, when it immediately tried to bite the young man. In astonishment he jumped back out of harm's way, shouting.

"Stop, stop! What are you trying to do?"

The animal, which was a snake, paused. Answering ever so coolly.

"I am going to bite you."

"How can you do this? I have just saved your life!"

"Well, that issss the way thingssss are with snakessss you ssssee, we bite."

"Oh no! Let us counsel with the otherwise animals first."

"Oh, yessss. But with whom?"

Snake smiled. You see, in the animal kingdom, there must be a counsel decision of three, on all matters of dispute where the best of three wins.

"How about Hyena? Let me remember, I saw him somewhere on my way here."

The young man volunteering in eager anticipation, they went to find Hyena. Suffice to say Snake's smile grew even bigger. On finding Hyena, they counselled with him. The young man, because it was his turn, explained what happened between him and Snake. Well, Hyena may not be the wisest animal in the bush. But he knew a good thing when he saw one, knowing after Snake had bitten the young man, he could eat him too. See what I mean?

"What would it matter if you were bitten?"

Answered the grinning Hyena, with a few underhanded chuckles at the end.

"Ssssee!"

Snake instantly slid up close to bite the young man. Once again, jumping back, the youth cried out his defence.

"Three... there must be three!"

"Three whatssss?"

Spat Snake, pulling up short.

"Three wise ones. Only by a majority of three wise ones can a matter be settled in the animal kingdom. You should know jungle law by now."

"I know jungle law, but I wassss unaware you did. That issss fine, because you are down one right now, sssso the next two you have to win. Who issss next?"

Snake, with his silly smile growing even larger than before.

"Isss my choice thisss time, I will choossse."

SURPRISE GUEST

AT THAT MOMENT WHO should appear, but Jackal, looking all fluffy and happy.

"Hello, all, why so gloomy?"

Snake started speaking to him about the situation they were facing. But Jackal interrupting him, before he could go into detail. Preferring to ask the young man his version first instead. The young man realising it was correctly Snake's turn, asked Snake's permission to address Jackal first. Snake nodded. Then the young man told Jackal the whole story, from the beginning as it had happened. Jackal laughed, remarking it could not be so, proceeded to walk on again. Snake butted in, insisting to Jackal it was indeed so, just as the young man had told him. Turning back to face them both, Jackal this time, addressed Snake.

"Why, why I do not believe this of you, Snake. You, covered by a rock you could not wriggle out from under, impossible. Unless I saw it for myself, I will not believe it."

"We will show you."

Exclaimed both Snake and the young man together.

"Well, lead away, show me the place, so I can be an impartial judge in this matter."

Arriving at the spot where the incident occurred, the two pointed out the rock to Jackal.

"Snake, slither over here, then let yourself be reintroduced to this rock once more. Let us see this matter through"

Snake was thinking in overtime. Believing for sure Jackal was on his side, being an animal and all. He had nothing to lose because when they rolled the rock off him again, he wins.

With this clear in his mind, Snake came boldly up to the rock, laying still while Jackal and the young man rolled the rock back over his head.

"Oh, so this is how it happened. Come, young man, we can be on our way."

After a while under the rock, Snake realised he had been tricked by Jackal, twisting, wriggling, every which way he could, to get out from under that rock, but to no avail.

NATURE PLAYS BY ITS OWN RULES

THE YOUNG MAN, LOOKING back felt sorry for Snake, wanting to roll away the rock once more. But cunning old Jackal stopped him this time.

"There you go again, with your morals. Look, in nature, if you are let free, you attack or eat what you see, especially if you are hungry or bad-tempered. You do not owe anyone a moral favour for being set free. Speaking of morals. It was Snake's own fault for believing in your and my morals, thinking we would set him free again. Did anyone tell him he would be set free? No! If you roll away the rock setting Snake free, you will have lost the vote. Snake can then bite you, by the rules of jungle law that is. Anyhow, was it not Snake, who without gratitude wanted to bite you after you freed him in the first place? That, my young friend, is murder in your world. No. Let Snake find his own way out from under that rock, as I am sure he will. It may take a little time, but he will. That is nature. In future young man, if you want to help something, be sure you know what you are helping first. I will be on my way, so I bid you farewell."

"Farewell to you too Jackal. Thank you for a well-learned lesson. What is more, I owe you my life. Thank you for that too."

"I will see you around young man. If there be anything I need, I will ask you."

With this conclusion, both went back to their original destinations, leaving Snake to fight his own battles.

The moral of the story, you say? God always forgives, man sometimes forgives, but nature never forgives.

CHAPTER 9

HOW THE LEOPARD GOT HIS SPOTS

Long, long, ago somewhere in Africa, when all the people and animals were new. Leopard, Lion and Hyena were the same colour as Lion is today. Then one day, Leopard and Hyena became spotted, but for different reasons.

This tale is, of course, about Leopard with his spots, although the spots of Hyena cannot be ignored. This is because of the way Hyena became spotted, which had much to do with Leopard. Lion, as you will see, is another story.

Our tale begins with Hyena because of what he did to change the fortunes of history. Anyone knows, Hyena was a most unfortunate animal, in that he was not the most attractive to look at. Adding to this misfortune, Hyena and Lion were ceaselessly quarrelling over food and territory.

Lion, as you know, was the great king of all the beasts, so you can understand how this quarrelling caused an uncomfortable disturbance for him, and most of the other animals. The creatures less affected were Elephant, who was too big, Crocodile, who was too wet and Hippo also.

Lion, being the King of all the Beasts, was respected for his greatness, his strength, stout presence, good looks, powerful roaring voice, and his majestic stately bearing, true to a king. Added to this Lion, as you know, was wise.

Naturally, Hyena possessed none of these grand attributes, although, the great favour given to him by his maker was something to remember. If ever there was a gift to grant a meat-eating animal, Hyena was given the singularity of having the most powerful jaws of any mammal in Africa.

Unfortunately, he did not use his gift wisely, developing a most disrespectful attitude toward Lion, constantly bothering him when he was eating. Hyena misused his powerful jaws in this way, thinking he could steal the big cat's food or simply worry him away from it. Likewise, he used this ploy against other meat-eating creatures he happened upon, including Leopard.

Demonstrating his bullying nature one day, Hyena, for no real reason other than his natural bad temper, put Tortoise up into the fork of a tree. Tortoise, obviously, had no way of getting down from that tree and Hyena knew it. He objected bitterly to Hyena, warning that some bad thing would come upon him if he did not stop behaving like this. Ignoring Tortoise's objections and admonitions, Hyena laughed to himself as he continued on his way, looking to bother some other unsuspecting helpless animal he might chance upon, leaving Tortoise firmly stuck in the crook of that tree.

Now Tortoise was beautifully marked, with even designs all over his shell, which was actually his home. This hardshell gave protection from other animals hurting him. It was also a shelter against the fierce African weather, keeping Tortoise cool in the hot summer days and well-protected against the cold winter nights. Therefore, it would stand to reason, he loved his handsome shell and looked after it ever so nicely.

Of course, Tortoise's shell was finely fashioned by the creator, having specially shaped sections joining one another in symmetrical patterns. He, being a gifted artist, painted his home with radiant markings, making himself a truly attractive looking animal indeed. Everyone who knew and loved Tortoise recognised him for being a quiet, kind creature, bothering no one. For this reason and because he was so small, the other animals looked out for his wellbeing except, of course, Hyena.

LEOPARD GETS HIS SPOTS

MANY HOURS HAD COME and gone while poor Tortoise struggled in vain to free himself from the fork of the tree where Hyena had stuck him. It was purely by chance Leopard went out looking for food that day, and in his seeking, he passed by the tree in which Tortoise was stuck. Leopard, seeing Tortoise struggling up in the tree was most surprised.

"Tortoise, I did not know you also climb trees?"

Tortoise at this stage was extremely weary from his struggles to get out of that tree. Almost at his wits-end, he had been there for what seemed to him a long, long time. When hearing Leopard, he peered down at him mournfully.

"No Leopard, I cannot climb trees and I have no need to even be in a tree!"

"So, Tortoise, if you do not climb trees, how then did you end up so well-stuck in this tree?"

"Hyena put me here, and no matter how hard I try, I am unable to climb down,"

"Hyena is a bad lot, stealing food from me many times in the past."

Leopard, so saying, took Tortoise out of the tree, placing him back on the ground.

This true survivalist, a clever and skilful hunter, had his food regularly stolen from him by Hyena. Nevertheless, way back in the early days, Leopard decided to make an end of Hyena's tactics, by teaching himself to climb trees while carrying his food. At the same time, he learnt to use his claws to go straight up the tree vertically, with only his teeth to carry a whole antelope onto a high branch.

Leopard's purpose was to take his food beyond the reach of other meat-eating animals, especially Hyena, even when jumping. In this way, he could eat his meals in peace, way up in a tall tree. Whereupon, after his meal, Leopard would lie on a branch to have a nap without being bothered by anyone, while he kept an eye on his food.

Tortoise, being an artist of no small degree, offered to paint Leopard, out of gratitude for rescuing him.

"For helping me Leopard, I can paint you in a wonderful way. Would you like me to make you beautiful?"

To this kind offer, Leopard readily agreed, knowing what great skill Tortoise had as an artist. Immediately, Tortoise went to work on Leopard's tawny coloured hide. He did so by painting him with spots. Not any kind of spots, mind-you, these spots were the same kind as those of Tortoise himself.

On Leopard though, these spots matched one another in a most special way, as a result of what Tortoise said to them while painting.

"Where your neighbour is good, be you also good."

These words Tortoise spoke to Leopard's spots as he painted, giving Leopard an extraordinary glow and sparkle when he walked.

When Tortoise was finished, Leopard, looking at himself, felt rather proud. Thanking Tortoise, he went off straight away to show his friends, as well as the other animals. As Leopard went along his way, everyone he met admired and marvelled at him, wanting to know how he became so colourful.

"Who has made you so good-looking?"

Leopard told them the tale of how Hyena wedged Tortoise up in the fork of a tree, purely because of his bad temper. He told them how he came across Tortoise this way, then took him down and put him back on the ground again.

"For this kindness, Tortoise offered to paint me with this beauty, to which I agreed."

Before this day, Leopard, who lived in peace with all, was without fear from man or beast, moving freely among all he came across, except of course for Hyena. Life was going to change for Leopard, in ways he could not for a moment have imagined, especially since he became so beautiful. It was a proud and happy leopard that went around, showing the whole district how he had changed. All because of what the gifted, crafty, Tortoise had done for him.

Every animal who saw him wondered at him. Naturally, no one recognised him in his new colours. After telling them, one by one, who he was, Leopard became more and more liked by everyone who knew him, although he was already popular anyway.

On his way, he found his good friend Lion, whom he most looked like before he got his new spots. Lion jumped when he saw him, caught unexpectedly, in Lion's opinion that is. Thinking this was a new creature come to compete in his world, he was not amused. He was completely ready to defend himself, never mind, to protect his hunting grounds of old as well, no matter what the cost. Leopard stopped in his tracks, amazed by Lion's reaction forcing him to approach with caution.

"My friend, why do you look at me like this, like you want to attack me?"

"Who are you?"

"I am Leopard, your friend."

"So why did you come sneaking up on me like that then?"

Leopard was surprised Lion was acting in this way. He had not sneaked up on him. Besides, he just then told him who he was.

"You may not recognise me, but you must be accustomed to my voice by now!"

"I do not understand, the voice sounds familiar, but how do I know you are indeed Leopard? Have you seen yourself lately?"

"Yes, I am Leopard! I know I am now full of spots ..."

"You wait, Leopard is my friend, who is in fact, the same colour as me. Not some other crafty spotted creature pretending to be Leopard, trying to steal my kingdom."

"No, it is truly me, Leopard, your friend. And yes, I was the same colour as you, as you said, and no, I do not want your domain. I was trying to tell you, today Tort..."

"Enough!"

Once again, Lion, moving forward indicated for him to stop right that instant. Leopard trailed off, this time moving backwards, observing Lion's increasingly aggressive manner towards him.

Lion was not going to fall for this story from some sweet-talking, fancy spotted pyjama cat with teeth and claws, come to steal his realm. Besides, he had a position to uphold as king of the beasts. Therefore no usurper was going to steal his empire away from him. Especially not a sneaky spotted cat like this one.

With this clear in his mind, Lion stood fast, aggressively facing this new foe. Carefully perceiving Lion's actions, Leopard became most concerned with his friend's unfamiliar attitude towards him. Once again, cautiously moving back a pace or two, Leopard hoped in this way to indicate to Lion, he had no aggression towards his old friend. This had turned into a big misunderstanding between him and Lion.

It was obvious to Leopard this moment needed a wise approach. Seeing his friend was wise and not easily given to treachery. Leopard had an idea to save their friendship and in the doing, his own skin as well, of which by now he had become particularly partial to. This called for fast thinking on Leopard's part. Solemnly looking at Lion, he suggested.

"If I present you a riddle Lion, to which only you and I know the answer, would this convince you?"

"I do not think a riddle is going to alter your or my purposes, so before we get into a fight for territory, I think we should go our separate ways, till I find the Leopard I know."

Leopard turned and went his way, leaving Lion to work things out for himself. He was convinced Lion would soon come looking for him, then at that time, he would have to face the facts. Aside from Lion, Leopard's traumas were far from over. Unbeknown to him, life was soon to take another strange new direction.

THE HOEING PEOPLE

LEOPARD HAD BECOME a truly eye-catching animal, especially when seen for the first time. So, one day, Leopard remembered he had not shown himself to the village's roundabout. Consequently, down the pathway, he ambled to the nearby village, where the people knew him well. They had seen him pass by many times before while hoeing in their vegetable fields. On this occasion, they were peacefully at work when he passed them by. He nearly jumped out of his newly painted skin when they cried out with one voice.

"Oh, the beauty! Let us catch it and tie it up."

With a great fright, Leopard saw the villagers charging down at him brandishing sticks and hoes, screaming. He fled for his life into the forest to hide, never to return where the villagers lived, ever again. Suddenly, for no understandable reason, Leopard found himself hiding from all people who came to the forest, thinking they were chasing him. This was a point he really would have wanted to work out with his friend Lion.

Later, lying quietly in his tree, Leopard was reflecting on his recent encounter with Lion. He missed his long-time friend's companionship, being the only other animal like himself. Before long, Leopard, deep in thought, caught sight of movement in the undergrowth. There, slinking by, was none other than Hyena, who looked up to see this beautifully coloured spotted cat in Leopard's tree. He stopped dead in his tracks looking up.

"Whatever has happened? Are you actually the leopard I know?"

Leopard for a moment, considered denying it was he. Thereby, possibly he could rid himself of this most bothersome quadruped. Sighing, he answered, disgruntled at the fact he should be revealing himself to Hyena.

"Yes, it is me,"

"How did you get to be full of spots like that?"

Once again, Leopard pondered, taking no notice of Hyena's queries but something prompted him to reconsider.

"I was painted like this."

"Oh. Who then was it? Who has made you so fine-looking?"

"It was Tortoise after I took him out of the tree where you put him. As gratitude for rescuing him, Tortoise offered to paint me, as you see me now."

"Ooh, let him beautify me too. Where is he?"

Leopard hesitated to reveal the whereabouts of Tortoise. But on quick reflection, he reconsidered, deciding it might be a good idea.

"He is down towards the river. Be careful not to hurt him."

Hyena went straight to Tortoise. Before arriving, he had already made up his mind to play another trick if Tortoise should refuse his request.

"Tortoise, make me beautiful like you made Leopard beautiful!"

As you are aware, Hyena also had a tawny hide like Leopard and Lion, but the main difference was his fur was terribly motley and ill-kempt. Tortoise was fully aware of the nature of Hyena, in that he would play another cruel trick on him if he refused. On the other hand, seeing his chance to right some of the wrongs Hyena had foisted on so many unsuspecting animals, he agreed.

"Come,"

Tortoise immediately began painting Hyena, saying to each one of his spots, under his breath.

"Where your neighbour is a bad lot, be you too a bad lot."

"Stop muttering to yourself,"

Snapped Hyena, showing his impatience by rushing Tortoise along. When Tortoise stopped painting, he told Hyena to go to the place where the people were hoeing in their fields, to show himself off. Hyena brashly brushed Tortoise aside as he left, going happily straight down the path, to flaunt himself where the villagers were working. But, while Hyena was sauntering by the field, he saw a big stick come flying past his nose. It was the villagers chasing him, brandishing sticks and hoes.

"That is an evil thing! Kill! Kill! Kill!" Hyena ran for all he was worth, deep into the forest.

HYENA'S SEARCH FOR TORTOISE

THIS WAS NOT WHAT HYENA had expected as he disappeared into the bush, loudly proclaiming to anyone who would listen.

"I will smash Tortoise today, wherever I find that little beast. Before, I had merely stuck him up in a tree-fork. That was nothing. Wait till I find him this time!"

At this, he burst out at the spot where Tortoise painted him but found no sign of him anywhere. Meanwhile, Tortoise had been helped by Aardvark, going down Aardvark's hole in an ant-heap.

Leopard heard the ruckus. Knowing Hyena for the bad sort he was, he went looking for Tortoise. When he found his friend with Aardvark, Leopard assured him not to be afraid of Hyena anymore, seeing many animals in the kingdom were looking out for him, even more than before.

In his frantic searching, Hyena stumbled into Lion, nearly coming a cropper from a powerful right paw.

"Who are you? I cannot remember seeing you around these parts before,"

Lion growling at his intruder. Heh, that is a funny one, thought Hyena to himself. I think my new design may suit my future purposes decidedly well, in fact. In the meantime, his overactive mind conjured up too many schemes as he answered Lion.

"Ahem, I am a visitor passing through. I say, you would not by any chance have a tasty morsel for a traveller to chew on about these parts, now would you?"

"Who is wanting to know? And what is your name? You still have not answered my first question."

"Oh, I am travelling through these regions, and if there be any meat to eat, I may stay."

"Meat? Stay? I never heard anyone inviting you!"

Hyena began to slink away. Recognising the big cat's irritation, he was well motivated to make tracks. This mannerism of Hyena's immediately alerted Lion, who instantly sprang forward, almost scaring the newly-painted spots off of Hyena.

"Hold on, hold on. I am Hyena."

"If you are Hyena, how come you are spotted all of a sudden?"

"Aaa, I think that is none of your business."

Moving fast, he headed deeper into the forest, seeking its protection from Lion, whom he could see was not in a good mood.

"Something strange is going on around here, with animals suddenly coming out in spots everywhere."

Irritated, Lion mumbled to himself, deciding right then and there to get to the bottom of these strange changes. He ventured off to find Leopard, his old friend, whom he had not seen in a while, to see if maybe he could shed some light on the subject.

LION CONSULTS LEOPARD

WHEN HE ARRIVED AT his old friends' tree, he looked up. Instead of finding a plain coloured Leopard as he expected, Lion found that spotted cat in Leopard's tree, which only made him more bewildered.

"Who are you? What are you doing in Leopard's tree?"

Leopard, hearing Lion's voice was pleased, thinking maybe his friend had come to his senses, wanting to talk. But, he was surprised by Lion's questions.

"Listen, I am aware we have had this discussion before. But I just now saw a hyena with spots much like yours, although somewhat ugly. Can you enlighten me as to why? I remember you offered me a puzzle explaining your case. Since I see you in Leopard's tree, and a spotted hyena going about these parts, I believe it is time for some kind of explanation."

Leopard climbed down from out of his tree, to better explain to a highly confused Lion, what had happened. Even before Leopard opened his mouth, Lion was urging him for the mystery.

"Give me that riddle you started when we last spoke, so I may come to grips with how this could have happened. My kingdom is turning into a circus right before my eyes."

Leopard, somewhat amused, nodded his head motioning for Lion to relax.

Lion slowly settled down, resting his head on his paws, as he listened to the explanations from this spotted cat.

Leopard thought he would try one more angle with Lion before using the mystery.

"Lion, of all the animals, who is the one both you and I have the most trouble from?"

"Ah, I think you should tell me. Otherwise, if I tell you, all you have to do is agree. How will that solve my problem?"

As you can see, Lion was wise, not easily fooled or persuaded.

"This riddle is meant to prove to you, I am actually the Leopard, you know."

"Let me hear the riddle, then I can decide."

"Alright, as I said before, only you and I are aware of the answer to this conundrum. The mystery must, therefore, be presented without letting on the name of our enemy for the puzzle to work. Considering you are sagacious Lion. Tell me in your wisdom, which animal would be able to paint another animal as well as I have been painted? He is also the one who painted himself."

"I cannot know if indeed you have been painted at all. Although, more to the question, there is only one of the animals who can paint as well as you could have been painted, who is also the one who painted himself, which is Tortoise.

What puzzles me, though, is why he would paint you in the first place. Besides, if you are Leopard, why would you let him? What further mystifies me, is who painted Hyena in such an ugly manner? Surely, that could not have been Tortoise, if he painted you so well?"

"The reason 'why,' is in the answer to the mystery."

Leopard continued to present his riddle, watchfully observing Lion and his responses, remembering only too well, their last encounter.

"I saved Tortoise from a terrible fate, by removing him from the crook of a tree where he was stuck. One of the animals put him there because, you see, Tortoise does not climb trees. Solving the name of the one, who put him there, should resolve the riddle for you, and at the same time answer your question 'why' as well,"

Lion, straightening up on his haunches, thoughtfully considering Leopard's conundrum. After a moment's contemplation, he needed no more prompting. He knew the answer. Looking intently at Leopard, he delivered a stately announcement.

"Well, only one would be so cruel as to put little Tortoise in a tree that way. He is an enemy of both you and me. His name is Hyena. And the 'why' you are painted, is because of Tortoise's gratitude for saving him out of the tree. Is that correct?"

Leopard nodded.

"That is what happened to you, but what came over Hyena, for him to get those hideous looking spots?"

When Leopard explained Hyena's story, Lion rolled over with laughter. Leopard, musing quietly to himself, was impressed by Lion's concern for his kingdom. At the same time, he realised his conundrum had saved their friendship.

With this happy outcome, Leopard, in his dazzling new spotted hide and Lion in his goodly old tawny one, ambled side-by-side, down the sandy riverbed, back to Lion's den, friends once more.

Nowadays, when people see Leopard's descendants, they marvel at their beauty. There again, when people see Hyena's descendants, they shudder.

The moral of the story, you say? It is said, many good things come from a good deed. But, one evil deed follows upon another, leading to ruin.

CHAPTER 10

THE CARPENTER AND THE LEGUAAN

Long, long, ago somewhere in Africa, when all the people and animals were new. A carpenter went to hunt for food, taking his faithful dogs along to help in his endeavours.

To begin with, things were not going too favourably, areas he knew to usually have an abundance of wildlife to pick from, failed him on this occasion. He decided before the sun grew too hot, it would best be for him to cross the river, an area he knew was well stocked with game. A hunting ground he did not visit too often, due to the river crossing, which presented added predators to face, like hippos and crocodiles. Food was scarce at home, thus good fortune was necessary, if he, along with his dogs, were to prosper in keeping up their strength.

Nearing the river, his dogs ran ahead of him, kicking up some dust as they ran off the track, stopping at the water's edge where they began barking at something a little way from the bank into the river. Approaching with caution, he found a leguaan half-hidden in the reeds on the river's edge. This was a fine hefty specimen of a creature. Slowly, quietening his dogs, he moved closer to get a better look at this handsome beast. But a surprise awaited him.

"Sir, do not kill me, further, please keep your dogs at a safe distance."

"How is it you speak, moreover, how is it I can hear you?"

"To some people, the gift of hearing wild creatures speak falls upon them, I perceived you were one of those. This is how we animals communicate with one another, or the animal kingdom would be in a chaotic state. Your gift I imagine comes from living a quiet life close to nature. What is your trade?"

"I am a carpenter making furniture from dead wood I find in the forest."

"Well, there you are then. Your closeness with nature has given you a gift."

"I see. Why can I not talk to my dogs then."

"Your dogs have become more human in nature, therefore they lose the ability to speak to humans."

"You are an amazingly wise creature. Where did you learn to be so wise?"

"Wisdom is sometimes a gift, yet sometimes learned. Mine is a gift."

"What an experience I have had. Thank you. No, I will not harm you. Sorry to have troubled you, we will be leaving now. Goodbye, stay well till we meet again."

"Sir, before you leave, I beg of you a favour. My tail is injured and as a result, I am unable to cross this river unaided. My tail is the usual means by which I manoeuvre myself in the water. Since it is injured, I am requesting if you will be so kind as to carry me across to the other side on your back. Your goodwill to me will earn you my indebtedness. For which I will pay you back some day when I am well again."

The carpenter obliged the heavy leguaan, carrying him on his back with no small effort on his part, all the way till he reached the other bank of the river. There, he let him go, then set forth to resume his task of hunting.

"Sir, your kindness will not go unrewarded. May I enquire where you stay?"

"I, with my dogs, live in a small hut where the tall palm trees grow, not far from where we met you."

"I know the place. When my tail has mended, I will make a visit. Also, because I am accustomed to this area, I suggest you follow the pathway to your right, where you will find what you are looking for. Thank you for your kindness."

"Till we meet again, best of healing for your tail."

It was a happy enlightened carpenter who went on with his hunt that day. Things turned out precisely as the leguaan had told him, it was not long before he found a small buck, which he killed. Taking it back home, he cooked dinner for himself, and his two dogs as usual.

THE WATCHMAN'S HUT

IN AFRICA, MONKEYS, wild pigs, hippos and elephants are the crop grower's biggest enemies. For this reason, watch huts are built out around the farmers' fields to keep away these wild beasts from destroying their food supplies at night time.

In the late summer, is the best time to hunt guineafowl, before the flocks break up. It is then, their internal parasites are less than in full summer. It was on one of these days the astute carpenter went out to hunt. He went to the region the leguaan told him about, having made it his regular hunting ground, because it was there, he met with his greatest success. Not long after arriving with his dogs, they soon found and killed five guineafowl. Hanging the birds from a stick over his shoulder, he made his way back to his hut. He was not far down the road when, out of the blue, enormous fast-moving thunder clouds blew in overhead. No sooner did they form together, when lightning began to strike ahead of the rain.

Quickly, thinking of one of the watcher's huts nearby, the carpenter ran to get cover, there to wait till the rain subsided before he continued his journey. Unbeknown to him, the leguaan he helped cross the river, had gotten the same idea a short while earlier, heading to the little hut for cover, he climbed up into the thatch where he lay well hidden from sight.

WHO EATS WHO?

TO MAKE THE BEST USE of his time, the carpenter sat down on a grass mat left there for resting on during long night watches.

Taking full advantage of the hut's protection, he began plucking the birds while he waited for the storm to pass. Before he had gone far with his chore, a lion sneaked up from behind him. When the dogs growled, he saw the lion. Jumping forward together with his dogs to escape the lion. But the lion scowled at them with a menacing look.

"Give your guineafowl to your dogs to eat, when they finish, you eat the dogs, then I will eat you."

The carpenter was terrified, as were his dogs, who cowered down behind him. The carpenter could neither speak nor move, being rooted to the spot with fright. He had hung up his bow with its arrows on a peg above his spear, which were then behind his attacker. The lion, receiving no response from the frightened carpenter, roared out the same words a second time.

"Listen, give your guineafowl to the dogs, so they may eat them, you eat the dogs, then I will eat you!"

Without warning, there came a booming voice from out of the thatch above them!

"Just so. Give the guineafowl to the dogs to eat. You eat the dogs. The lion will eat you. Then I will eat the lion."

The lion flattened himself hard down onto the ground, looking up, seeing nothing, he streaked out of that hut as fast as his legs would carry him. Never once looking back, with his tail between his legs. Making a beeline straight through the rain and lightning directly for the safety of the forest.

Only then did Leguaan reveal himself to the overjoyed carpenter together with his dogs.

"I did say, the day will come when I would return the kindness you afforded me. I am pleased it was on such an occasion."

"Thank you, Leguaan. That was a close encounter, I hope never to see again. From this moment on, my weapons will remain forever at my side when I go hunting."

The moral of the story, you say? Never underestimate your opponent, he may have friends in high places.

CHAPTER 11

HOW MANTIS GAVE THE BUSHMAN FIRE

Long, long, ago somewhere in Africa, when all the people and animals were new. There lived a people, amongst the creatures, who were extraordinarily cunning, crafty and skilful hunters. Considering these people hunted simply for what they needed, their labours were fruitful.

But when they would take the meat back to the tribe, it was eaten as the lion and the leopard would eat, always raw. You see, the people had no fire, nothing to light up the dark of a moonless night, or warm themselves in the bitter desert cold nights. Certainly, no fire to cook their food with. In fact, they never even thought of fire for themselves.

Do not get me wrong, they knew what lightning was, with the fire it made. But the fire which could be kept to be used when needed was not yet known.

This was a mission for Mantis. I am sure you have heard of Mantis, he sits on grasses, trees and flowers, mostly praying while waiting for his food to arrive. Mantis was a quiet, wide-eyed observer, studiously watching the goings-on around him with great patience.

It was the habit of clever Mantis to venture into places where no one even considered going before. Mostly he flew from destination to destination, yet sometime for the sheer adventure, he would walk. Wherever he went, he would watch and observe closely the things he saw. He was ever curious, ponderously pondering problems encountered by his fellow-creatures for hours. Sometimes Mantis would dream the dreams wise-ones dreamed. In those dreams, he would see remedies for many dilemmas encountered by his fellow nature dwellers.

Sadly, the problem mostly troubling Mantis was the plight of the people. The people with no fire. They saddened Mantis. If only the people had fire, for comfort in winter, light in the darkness, to cooked food when they needed to. It would brighten their lives in the many ways his dreams had revealed.

While he was observing, the people eating raw food one day, a vision came to him. He saw Ostrich, the food he ate, how it smelled. Even one day, when he dropped a piece, he tasted it. It tasted better than any food Mantis ever experienced before. Of course, that was his answer, Ostrich, must have fire. But how was he going to get it?

WHERE DID OSTRICH GET HIS FIRE?

MANTIS, OFTEN WONDERED why the food, which Ostrich ate would smell so different, so delicious, he must use fire to cook it. Mantis had a mission to get fire from Ostrich for the people. Many years back, while observing Ostrich, he noticed how he would go off somewhere hidden to eat his food.

But the big mystery was, where did Ostrich get this fire from? It was hard to approach Ostrich on account of his secretive nature. Mantis was not one to give up easily, though. Over a long time of watching Ostrich, Mantis learned anytime his fine feathered friend came to eating his tasty food, he had shortly before gone missing for some time. Mantis decided, now was the time to find out where he went and where he kept the fire.

Having made up his mind to give the people fire, he was determined to discover the fire of Ostrich. Setting himself the task to find the fire or bust, he started by following Ostrich around at his meal times. Carefully observing Ostrich day after day, Mantis noticed how he ever looked behind himself, stopping continuously, suspiciously, searching to see if anyone was following him, before moving on any further. Only moving on, when he was confident the coast was clear, in a manner of speaking.

It was going to be hard to follow Ostrich without being found out. Therefore, Mantis devised a plan to beat Ostrich at his own game.

From a distance, well-hidden, he marked each turn Ostrich took till where he lost sight of him. The following day, he would wait in hiding at the precise spot where Ostrich was last seen by him the day before. It was there, he would hide, waiting at the expected time Ostrich would pass by. Day after day, he moved to a new spot where he last saw Ostrich the day before. Each day, he did the same thing, patiently waited in hiding for Ostrich to pass by. This went on for some time, till the day Mantis saw Ostrich go up a high kopje, then through thick bush surrounded by tall trees. Mantis was resolved, this must surely be the spot where Ostrich made his fire.

The following day, taking up his new position where Ostrich disappeared through the tall trees the day before, Mantis waited. When Ostrich passed by disappearing into the trees, he went closer. There he saw it, it was perfectly hidden, any passer-by would not know such a place could exist. Mantis remembered a time, not too long before, when he was looking for Jackalberries in this region he never even noticed the scene he now faced.

There as clear as day, in the middle of the trees and shrubs, was a circled clearing, well hidden from any prying eyes. Mantis carefully, slowly closing in, saw in the middle of the clearing a group of rocks burnt black, wood ash strewn from the black stones to the surrounding bushes. Judiciously studying his surrounds, he was able to see why this was such a cleaver place to make a fire because the tall trees with those low, dense shrubs would hide the smoke. Further, being high on a hillock, the smallest breeze would blow away any trace of smoke, which would appear above the trees. Mantis was extremely impressed with the craftiness with which Ostrich hid his fire. But mystery of mysteries, where did he keep it?

Closer, he watched in amazement as Ostrich furtively reached beneath his one wing pulling out the fire. Taking the fire, he lit up the sticks that were laid on the rocks before him. From under his other wing came the food, which the crafty bird placed on the fire and proceeded to cook it. When he was finished with lighting up the sticks, he replaced the fire, tucking it back under his wing once more. Mantis watched until he was satisfied, then unseen, he slipped quickly away when Ostrich got busy eating his cooked food.

THE JACKALBERRY FRUIT

HOW LONG OSTRICH HAD hidden this secret of the fire, no one knows. One thing Mantis was assured of, Ostrich would not share his fire willingly with anyone. This meant concocting a plan, which would of necessity, be resorting to trickery. Mantis reasoned this was the only way he was going to get any fire out of Ostrich for the people. In the interim, he bided his time while hatching his plan out properly in fine detail.

When the fruit of the Jackalberry tree ripened, it was Mantis' cue, things were ready for action. Mantis went to find Ostrich. While visiting, he sneakily mentioned an important fact to Ostrich in passing.

"By the way, did you know the Jackalberry tree is full of ripe fruit."

"Oh, goody, goody. Where?"

Well, we know how Ostrich loves Jackalberry fruit. Nothing and nobody could stop Ostrich from going to a Jackalberry tree with ripe fruit on it. Simply point in the general direction, for an instant result.

Ostrich was overjoyed, following Mantis as he led the way to the juicy Jackalberry tree. Sure enough, the tree was there, precisely as Mantis told Ostrich and it was as he said, full of ripe fruit. Ostrich began to eat with Mantis moving up, deeper into the tree, dancing away, muttering as he went.

"Here look at this, you are missing the best ones. Higher, no come higher, the sweetest ones are up at the top!"

Ostrich struggled and strained, but he simply wasn't tall enough.

"Step on that stone there, then hop onto this big branch here."

Gratefully using the rock, Ostrich stepped up, reaching out to the big branch on tiptoe, he spread his wings to balance himself. The perfect opportunity, quick-as-a-wink, Mantis grabbed some of the fire from beneath Ostrich's wing. Instantly, with a whirr and a click, he was gone, flying high into the sky.

Mantis took the fire directly to the people who lived amongst the creatures. That my friends, is how the Bushman got fire. But wait there is more.

Ever since then, Ostrich, greatly embarrassed, has never flown. He keeps his wings tightly pressed to his sides, to preserve the little fire he has left. As any Bushman will tell you, Ostrich and his wife have become a little absent-mindedly distracted, since the theft of some of their fire.

Even when mother ostrich lays her beautiful, creamy eggs in a warm hollow in the sand, Ostrich places one egg out in the open sand to remind them both they are sitting on a clutch of eggs, lest they forget and wander off.

If you go where the Ostrich lives today, you will always find the Ostriches egg marker, when they are sitting on their eggs.

The morel of the story, you say? There is nothing hidden that will not come to light.

CHAPTER 12

THE DAMSEL AND THE DRAGONFLY

Long, long ago, somewhere in Africa, when all the people and animals were new, there existed a watery paradise you may never have heard of. This water wonderland blossomed in the heart of a vast desert fed by great rivers, flowing down from the mountains and plains of central Africa.

This utopia, hidden in a vast network of small and large islands, was lushly decorated with palms, papyrus and forested trees. Interlaced with channels of crystal-clear flowing water, it formed a mighty inland delta. All kinds of animals, birds and insects called this home.

In the heart of this watery wonderland, dwelt the largest family of dragonflies in all of Africa. This was known to many as the land of the water nymphs.

It was there that a peaceful group of ochre-skinned people had settled. On one of the larger sandy, palm and tree-studded islands, where the water lilies grew in abundance, lived a boat builder, his wife and young daughter. Transport in this region was by hollowed-out tree boats, called makoros. While standing upright in these makoros, people navigated the waters by means of punting poles pushed onto the sandy bottom.

As the story goes, the young daughter was blessed with a special gift, of hearing and speaking to dragonflies. Standing at the water's edge, she would hear symphonies of sound from the dragonflies, which filled the sky and the overwhelming number of nymphs beneath the water. It was said, the sounds the damsel heard from these extraordinary number of creatures, were the dragonflies and nymphs talking one to another in musical tones. This may sound strange to you, but all nymphs and dragonflies communicate in this musical language.

Why so many dragonflies, you may ask? Well, dragonflies live chiefly off mosquitos and their lava, which also use water to breed. Therefore, it stands to reason, the dragonflies will be there.

Dragonflies feed by darting down to skim the water's surface, touching, touching, touching as they go. This is their feeding action, scooping up the mosquito larvae at the exact moment they come up to the surface of the water for air.

On fine sunny days, when the sun sends glittering shafts of light deep into the crystal-clear mountain water, one is able to see right into the nymph's underwater world. It was a day like this when a special secret was revealed to the young girl.

Our damsel loved to peer deep down between the flowers, which grew out of the sparkling desert sand at the bottom of the abundant water gardens. This was the watery world the nymphs inhabited, feeding amongst the flowers.

As usual, she tucked herself down on all fours in the warm sand, her nose to the water, oblivious to the rest of the world. There, our damsel stared at the nymphs swimming among the multi-coloured plants. On this occasion, she was distracted by movement at the base of a lily blossom, closer than an arm's length. Going nearer to inspect, she found to her surprise, it was a nymph, clinging tightly to a lily petal.

THE LADY MEETS A NYMPH

OH, HOW EXCITING! A nymph, out of the water. How strange, she thought to herself. She had been unable to talk to the nymphs under the water, although she had tried many times. She could hear them, but they were unable to hear her. The dragonflies were different, she could talk to them and they, in turn, could talk back. Here, for the first time, was her opportunity to maybe talk to a nymph, one who had come out of the water.

"Hello, can you hear me?"

"I can hear you, but only softly. My ears are coated with skin. Come a little closer."

"I see. And you can talk. I am so excited to be able to talk to you. But why are you at the top of the water, when your family is down at the bottom? I have never seen a nymph on the top of the water before."

"It is something which happens to nymphs when they get older and more mature."

"How old are you? And, are you male or female?"

"Oh, I am of a great age, more than a thousand suns and moons ago I was born. I am of the male gender."

"You sound sad. What is the matter?"

"I am going to die."

"Oh, no. What makes you think that?"

"This thing, which has happened to me, has happened to all of our aged nymphs over many moons."

"And what might that be?"

The old nymph began his story with a sigh. As he explained, anytime a mature nymph had the urge to go to the top of the water, the other nymphs would try to stop them. This had gone on for many generations since forever because when they leave their world down below, they never came back. The other nymphs came to believe they must have been eaten by something.

He was going to go back to tell his nymph family what it was like to be above the water if he lived to tell his tale. This was agreed between him and the others, for he promised he would keep his word. He would not be like the ones who had gone before, who never went back. Because they failed to keep their promise, the nymphs believed them to be dead. This happened even though they solemnly gave their word to go back.

"This is why I am afraid. So, if I live, I will keep my vow and go back."

"What is your name?"

"We nymphs have no name. We know one another by a soundwave. You see, each nymph has their pitch of sound they are known by. What is your name?"

"My name is Star. My father named me that because I was the brightest moment in his life when I was born."

"What a beautiful story. You must tell me more, but now I am unable to talk anymore. I have taken in too much air."

"Too much air? How come?"

"We nymphs living in the water, get our air from the water. But, since I am at the top out of the water, I must start to breathe air. Sorry, I must be quiet, till another sun and a moon have passed."

With that, the nymph stopped talking. Deep in thought, the sun streaming orange glows across the sky, Star slowly rose to her feet. Dusting sand from her hands and knees, she started back for home, in wonder of the days' events. At the cooking pots was Mother, preparing food before nightfall.

MOTHER HEARS THE STORY

STAR WAS AWFULLY EXCITED to have met this nymph since he was the first she had ever been able to talk to. She was like a chirping nightingale, hurriedly telling her mother the wonderful experiences of the day. But Mother interrupted before Star began her story in earnest.

"Come, sit back here next to me, where I can listen to you properly, away from the heat and the noise of cooking. The nymph story, I have heard from the wise men, but not as you are telling it. You, my young lady, are going to see it unfold right before your eyes, as none have before you. Tell me, does it speak? You have told me the nymphs are unable to hear you."

"Oh, yes. Since it's out of the water. But only softly, there is a skin covering his mouth and ears."

"You are going to experience a miracle of life and one spoken of by the elders of our people with awe, from as far back as we can remember."

"What is it? Tell me? Tell me, please?"

"No, my dear child, I will not. It will spoil your chance of viewing a wonder of creation in action. And I do not want to spoil your opportunity of seeing something truly extraordinary."

Star would have loved to tell her father, but he was away on a big hunt. The next day early, she was back to talk to the nymph, but he did not answer her the entire day. On the day after, from the early morning, our damsel kept a watchful eye on her nymph friend. At around noon, peering closely she saw the nymph's skin had become hard and dry. Not long after, a crack developed on the top of the nymph's back.

"My skin is cracking. It is cracking the whole way down my back. I can feel it."

"I have been here since early this morning. Are you alright?"

"I am fine, but I must press hard to push my body out of this dry skin."

Arching backwards, the nymph pushed and pushed, till he escaped his skin. Holding his chest high, he pulled out his legs from their casings, till all six were in the sun.

"Look, you have little wings on your back."

"I can feel them, but I cannot see them or move them. What does this mean?"

"I am not sure, but my mother said I was going to see a great wonder. Are you feeling alright?"

"I am feeling more than alright. I am free and light and warm all over."

"That is the sun. It is warming and drying you."

"I must breathe deeply to push myself free from this old skin before I dry folded up."

So, the nymph began to push as hard as he could. While he did this, his body freed itself completely from the old skin. Then he began to grow longer and longer, till he was three times what he was before. As he pushed, even more, his wings grew bigger and bigger, till his four wings were wider than he was long. Then he became afraid, and tears began to well up in his big round eyes.

"Oh, do not cry, you are a dragonfly. A beautiful shiny pale blue dragonfly, with the comeliest shimmering eyes. You have flecks of red covering your wings, like fine silk glittering in the sunlight. Oh, I am sorry, you have no idea what I am talking about."

"What is a dragonfly?"

"See the cloud of creatures flying around above and beyond you? They are dragonflies, all as beautiful as the next, as you are now."

"But they are flying and I am stuck down here on this flower."

"You must fly. Flap those wings. You have to join your kind in the sky."

The young dragonfly did what Star told him. With a zip, he was in the air. He flittered around, having the world of fun, before settling back down on the end of a twig, right next to his new friend.

"I am so happy. I am light and free. I can go anywhere I see."

TO KEEP A PROMISE

NO SOONER HAD HE SAID this when he remembered his nymph family and his promise to return. He took off past Star, diving for the water, bouncing right off, unable to penetrate its dense surface, even after trying over and over again. Saddened, he flew back to the twig next to Star.

"As happy as I am, I am sad I cannot pierce the water to tell my nymph family what a great thing has happened to me. Now I know, this is why the ones who promised to go back were unable to keep their word. Star, you speak to me. Can you not for me, speak to them?"

"Sorry, I have tried many times, but my voice is not heard where you used to live. The same thing is going to happen to them one day, as what has happened to you. And they will also start to understand what has happened, in the same way, you found out. It is the way things were created."

"I understand more clearly, but it will be a great joy for them when they discover their new destiny as I did. I see, the sun is going down to bed for the night and I must find a place to sleep."

"Meet me here in the morning when I come. Farewell and good night, I am going home to help my mother prepare the evening meal. Do not be sorrowful, be happy, my little friend."

Star went home, trembling with excitement. Straining to talk normally, she blurted out the wonderful things she had seen.

"Mother, you will find it hard to believe the amazing things I saw today?"

"Try me. I know more of the mysteries of nature than you may realise. But this sounds good, let us talk. Come, sit by the fire and tell me your story."

The moment they sat down, a group of fireflies appeared above them, scattering sparkling flashes of light as they flew back and forth in the evening sky. Could they also have come to hear Star's story of the dragonfly?

"Look, Star, is that not wonderful? They have come to hear your story. Go on, tell us what happened?"

"Today, when I came to the nymph, his skin had begun to crack and slowly, slowly, out came this shrivelled little creature. But, with much effort on his part, he began to grow and grow. Then with a final mighty struggle, he changed from a nymph into a beautiful dragonfly!

When he could fly, he tried to return to the water to tell his nymph family what had happened to him, but he could not get back into the water. Tell me, did you know dragonflies come from the nymphs living at the bottom of the water?"

"I did. It is this I kept from telling you the other day. You see, the skin they have to escape is much like our own. One day like the dragonfly, we must also leave this body so we can be free to join the Creator. Then, as the dragonfly left the water, we will leave this world, unable to return, much like the dragonfly tried but without success. Nor will we want to.

This day, my young daughter, you have learned the secret of the dragonfly our people have known for aeons of time. This is the secret of life and more life. Life, because we see, feel and live in this world. More life, because we leave this one for a better one, like the dragonfly."

Star looked up into the nighttime sky.

"Mother, maybe there is more to why father named me Star."

"Hmmm."

Deep in thought, Star's mother smiled to herself, pondering her daughter's story as she watched her staring up into the Milky Way.

The moral of the story, you say? If you waste the mysteries of today, you may miss the ones for tomorrow.

CHAPTER 13

JACKAL, LION AND THE FALLING ROCKS

Long, long, ago somewhere in Africa, when all the people and animals were new. Jackal was moseying – he moseyed a lot - along through a narrow, rocky passage between the hills. As was his habit, he kept his nose to the track while sauntering, checking for interesting smells, mumbling to himself as he went.

"Never know when or where my next meal may turn up,"

Although it was highly unlikely a rat or a fat little mouse would be out in such heat. Maybe, or even possibly, there would be a lizard or a lazy rabbit out and about, to snack on. Still, keeping his nose to the ground, he kept searching. Up to this point, Jackal's search had produced nothing on this extremely humid, hot summers day. No sooner was he ready to call it quits and go home, when he saw movement on the pathway up ahead. Who would be out on such a hot day, except another hungry hunter like himself?

"Oh, no!"

Jackal moaning froze in his tracks. Lion was moving directly towards him. Realising he surely must have been seen by Lion, he remained paralysed to the spot, on account of him being too close for escape. Jackal was terrified. He had played so many tricks on the old chap and some of them recently, it was certain Lion would take every chance to get his revenge.

When Jackal realised for sure Lion had seen him, he swallowed hard and in his fright, he instantly hatched a plan. He noticed, above him, along the pass, large, unstable looking rocks forming part of the cliff face, this gave him his out.

"Help! Help!"

Not looking in Lion's direction, but looking up at the rocks above, Jackal cried. He cringed down on the cliff path, to his right a certain death fall and on his left a sheer wall of rocks and in front, a black-maned lion bearing down on him. Jackal simply lay there head up, eyeing the rocks above, moaning to himself. His fear for Lion being the perfect motivator for the real fear he felt to aid the fraud he was perpetrating. Lion stopped short in surprise, first looking suspiciously at Jackal then behind himself.

"Help! Help!"

Jackal still not looking in Lion's direction howled, using all the fear he felt in the middle of his chest to put emphasis in his cry. Jackal created the impression he was crying to anybody who could hear him. Then, pretending to have just noticed Lion standing over him, he twisted his head to glance up, a pitiful look on his face. Perplexed, Lion stared back at him.

"Help! Oh, great One! Thank you for coming. I am glad you are here with your mighty strength. There could be no one better. There is no time to lose! See those huge rocks above us? They are slipping about to fall! We shall both be crushed to death! Oh, mighty Lion, do something! Please do something! Please save us!"

Jackal cowering even lower, covering his head with his paws.

LION CHECKS OUT THE ROCKS

LION LOOKED UP AT THE large rocks above him, suddenly becoming most alarmed. They certainly looked dangerously perched where they were. Before he even had a chance to think, Jackal was begging him once again. Suggesting he use his enormous shoulder strength to hold up the menacing rock closest to them.

"Oh, what an unkind way to die. Our children will never know what happened to us, squashed here under the rocks with no one to tell them. If you O King, put your powerful shoulder to this rock above me, we will be saved. In the meantime, I will go and find a support to prop it up to save you."

Lion put his muscled shoulder to the rock, then heaved.

"Quickly Jackal, move, go get the support."

"Oh, thank you, great King, thank you! I will quickly get a log to brace the rock, and we shall both be saved!"

With that, Jackal bounded away, out of sight, back the way he had come, leaving Lion alone to struggle under the weight of those immovable rocks. How long he endured with the rock, before he realised it was another hoax by Jackal, we will never know.

But this much we do know. Jackal escaped Lion many times in the past and still continues to live by his wits to this day!

The moral of the story, you say? Be cautious not to shoulder burdens in vain. Kindness is not always rewarded with a thankful end.

CHAPTER 14

THE CHIEF WHO WAS NO FOOL

Long, long, ago somewhere in Africa, when all the people and animals were new. There was a Chief of a large district, the ruler of many people, who became known for his wisdom far and wide. As the knowledge of him grew, more and more came to seek his great counsel, on matters hard to solve.

Yet there was a sudden change coming for this wise Chief, one he could never have dreamed possible. This happened on a day, a normal court day, like any other day, two men from his own district came seeking the great Chief's wisdom, on a simple matter of theft. The surprising events that were to transpire would lead to a new future for the Chief, in a most unexpected way.

As was said before, on this day, an old man with his younger neighbour approached the Chief for a solution in solving what they thought to be a simple case. When they were called forward to plead their case and being the elder, the old man correctly addressed the Chief first.

"Oh, wise Chief, thank you for hearing my case, I have been stolen from by this man, my neighbour. Therefore your wise help I have come to pursue."

The Chief nodded his approval to the old man, for being recognised as wise.

"You may proceed. Elaborate for me on the problem you are facing?"

"Chief, the case is simple. My neighbour knows I am a poor man yet still, he has stolen the few goats I had for milk for my food. I spent a long time searching for my goats, two full moons I searched, till I found them in this man's flocks. When I asked him for my goats back, he refused, saying they were his goats."

The Chief looked surprised, directing his question to the old man's neighbour.

"Is this old man telling the truth about you? How do you say?"

"No! He is making it all up. I do not need his goats, I have many goats of my own. How come it took him so much time to find them. After the much time he spent, I think he got tired of searching, then he decided to claim twelve of my goats."

"Have you counted your goats of late to see if maybe the old man is right?"

"Yes. I have a hundred and twenty-six since lambing season, which is before this man claimed I stole his animals."

The Chief had a long think regarding their problem, obviously not wanting the wrong man to be punished. He, in his wisdom, decided upon a riddle, reckoning the one who was innocent, would know the answer to this riddle he was about to pose, because of the matter contained in the conundrum.

"I need the answer to a riddle I have set for you both. The one who comes to me with the right reply first will receive all the goats. As to the question; I want to know the fastest thing in the world and why you think it is so."

With this, the Chief dismissed the two men.

The two men left the Chief's court, completely dumbfounded, neither one happy at the difficulty of the Chief's riddle.

THE WISE DAUGHTER

AS IT OFTEN IS WITH old people, they have large families. After pondering this strange question for a long time without a resolution. The old man's wife, seeing her husband struggling over the riddle without success, suggested he go talk to their wise daughter, the one with whom he never won an argument.

This daughter, Ziah by name, was not only wise but beautiful, known in their district for resolving many disputes. After hearing her father's riddle from the Chief, Ziah quickly told her father the answer.

First thing the next day, armed with this knowledge, the old man went boldly to the Chief's court. The Chief was more than a little surprised to see the old man back so soon. Therefore, with some amazement, he stared quizzically while he addressed him.

"Old man, can it be, that you have the answer to my riddle already?"

"O wise Chief, I hope I have not come to disturb you without good reason?"

"Well, let us see, say on, how is your answer to the fastest thing in the world and why it is so?"

"Time, O Chief, I humbly submit to you, is the fastest thing in the world. And the reasons, as you asked for. Are the years go by so quickly we cannot even remember all we have done in them. Time also goes too fast to finish the things we like to do. The speed of time cannot be measured for its mysteries."

Without a doubt, this solution came from an extremely wise person, well versed in literature. Therefore, the Chief seeing this simple man before him, had serious suspicions concerning this answer. He doubted it was the old man who came up with such a wise solution since he was not a learned man. The Chief, even questioned he could have given a better reply to the riddle himself. Reconciled to the fact it was beyond the old man standing before him to have such learning, he was determined to find out who in his kingdom possessed such wisdom.

"Old man, who did you consult, for so wise a resolve?"

Fear struck the old man, fear of losing his goats to his neighbour, fear for himself, then fear for his daughter getting into trouble. But instead, he persisted.

"O wise Chief, it was hard, but I studied your riddle for a long time before I worked out time was definitely the right answer. Remembering how much time I spent trying to find my own lost goats."

It was evident to the Chief, the old man was protecting the one who gave him the riddles' solution. The Chief also realised he was afraid, but he was determined to find the giver of such great wisdom.

"Old man, if you do not tell me the truth, I will punish you. Not the one who gave you the answer."

Hearing this, panic gripped the old man in another way this time. He would not only lose his goats but get his whole family into trouble as well, starting with himself. For this reason, he delayed answering the Chief, who was growing annoyingly impatient, waiting on the old man's answer.

"Well?" What is your answer?"

"I have a wise daughter whose name is Ziah, she gave me the explanation to the puzzle you set for me."

The old man was scared and relieved, all in one. Believing the Chief's promise, not to punish the one who gave him the answer. Pleased to get the whole thing off his chest.

"She is indeed a wise daughter, it would please me to meet her. The goats have become yours because of your daughter's wise answer. I will have your neighbour informed to bring you the goats. You may go."

It was an awfully relieved and happy old man who left the court that day.

THE PROPOSAL

DURING THE SPRING RAIN festival and amid much pomp and ceremony, the Chief met the old man's wise daughter Ziah, whom he invited to be his guest of honour. When Ziah was presented to the Chief, he was completely overtaken by the woman's absolute beauty.

The Chief could see, the finery of her clothes had little to compare within his whole land. Unknown to the Chief, these she made herself. Adding to her beauty, her conversation was filled with humility and knowledge. She, such a wise woman besides.

Many guests approached the Chief to compliment him on what a gracious companion he had in Ziah. Completely overcome with wonder for this woman, the Chief reasoned her to be a perfect match for him, deciding then and there to propose. Quickly, pursuing the old man, he requested Ziah's hand in marriage. Of course, the old man was enthralled, consenting to the Chief's desire. Without a moment to waste, the Chief was back to enquire of Ziah.

"My lady Ziah, I am persuaded by your striking beauty, your wise and gracious demeanour, notwithstanding your irresistible charm, to ask for your hand in marriage. All I own, I will share equally with you. I will be a faithful husband. All I ask in return is for one rule. You respect my courtroom, not to give private counsel without talking to me first. If you should break this rule, I will be forced to banish you from my court without compensation. Further, your father has consented to our union. Now would you honour me by accepting my offer, to be my wife for life? Before I find myself a fool when someone else does."

The wise Ziah smiled, bowing her head down low in courteous submission.

"I accept. You could be no fool, my wise Chief. I am the one honoured that I should become your wife."

A short time later amid huge celebrations, Ziah was married to the Chief in great opulence and pageantry befitting that of a king with his queen. The Chief was honoured by the guests' who showed him their well-founded admirations for Ziah.

After the wedding celebrations, the Chief one day, reflecting on the many guests who complimented him on the choice of such a wise wife. Remembering the private counselling she had given to many. Thought it prudent to remind her of their agreement in this matter.

"My husband, I would never break our agreement, besides you are the appointed leader of our people. Furthermore, as I am now your wife, I consider any private counselling outside of your court, not honourable. I acknowledge your superiority in all court matters to always be, outside of my dominion."

MANY YEARS LATER

THE YEARS PASSED BY, with the Chief continuing in his usual manner. Hearing all the people's needs and grievances who came to receive his wise counsel in matters that mattered.

On occasion, the Chief would even ask Ziah about a particular problem he found difficult to resolve. Ziah, always a kindly, thoughtful person, gave her husband wise counsel in ways which came across like the Chief thought of the solution himself. Although Ziah never involved herself in any of the Chiefs business, she did see some injustices in her judgement, but as a wise woman, she kept her silence in these matters.

All these things considered, there came a day where Ziah's patience, wisdom and obedience were sorely tried to the utmost. This happened with a particular case which recently came before the Chief, involving two teenagers, each claiming the other stole his sheep. Ziah knew most of the people in their local chiefdom, therefore in this instance, she was also aware of which one of the boys owned the sheep. For this reason, her heart went out to him.

This case unnaturally stretched out for some time. Yet every time the boys went to the Chief for his counsel, she would see them.

On this one day, when they left the court, they were both peering down at something in their hands. Ziah was watching out for them when she heard the one boy talking of the hard thing the Chief set for them.

Ziah was fully aware of her promise to her husband, remembering she was not to give private counsel to the people. Yet she waited for the boy who owned the sheep to be alone before she approached him.

When the right moment came, she quietly approached the innocent boy sitting on his own, elbows on his thighs, holding his head in his hands, looking down hopelessly forlorn at his foot, as he kicked at the sand. Ziah approaching quietly sat down beside him, then inquired of the problem he was facing.

"Young man, I have seen you come and go from the Chief a fair amount of times lately. May I enquire what troubles you."

"Chief has set an impossible task. He gave us each an egg, saying, whoever hatches it first by the next day will own the sheep. What does a chicken's egg have to do with my stolen sheep? That is why I am sitting here, lost for a solution for my sheep. I am also afraid."

Then Ziah patiently explained to the boy what was expected of him by the Chief, explaining the reason he set such a hard riddle.

"The riddle is not primarily to do with the egg. The Chief has made this riddle to distinguish who is the honest person among you two. The one who dares to return to reason with him, to prove the egg cannot be hatched in one day, will get the sheep. Since it proves to the Chief, that person is serious in getting a solution to his problem. Therefore, he must be the innocent one and in so doing, also the rightful owner. Further, by his sincere action, he deserves the sheep, knowing he cares for it and will also look after it."

"I cannot think to match the Chief's wisdom, so I am afraid to speak to him."

Ziah, in her wisdom, knew the solution to the boy's problem, but she dare not break her word. After careful consideration, she thought up a plan, without her having to break her promise to her husband. The sorrow she felt for the youth, persuaded her to help him.

"Apart from it being morally wrong, I am bound to keep a promise to the Chief, never to counsel any of the people in matters of court. In your case, without breaking my word, I am going to allow you to come up with the answer by yourself. First, let me ask you your thinking in connection with this problem you have. I want you to think it out for yourself."

"I think it is impossible to give such a stupid request to two young boys when it has nothing to do with who owns the sheep."

"All right, I am going to take that as an answer. You said it is impossible? What is impossible?"

"It is impossible to hatch the egg before tomorrow."

"Do you sincerely believe that?"

"Yes, I do."

"Why?"

"Because no one can hatch an egg in one day."

"Alright, is there anything else you know which cannot be done in one day?

"My father is a farmer. Therefore I know you cannot grow millet in one day."

"Good, I think you are getting the picture. If you were told to jump off a cliff, what would your answer be? Careful here, I want you to think it out, by applying reason."

"I would tell them to jump off the cliff themselves. Oh, I see. One statement cancels out the other. So, it is just as impossible to, to... to grow millet in one day as it is to hatch an egg."

"Exactly. That is how you think things out for yourself. Remembering your millet story, tell me what you think you need to say to the Chief, that relates to the riddle he set for you?"

"Well, I would ask him to get millet to grow in one day, so I can feed the greens to my chicken I must hatch in one day as well."

"There you are, you see, you came to the right conclusion all by yourself, without someone telling you. You see, that is what wisdom is all about. You must apply yourself to any problem by reason, not by chance."

"All right, what must I then say to the Chief tomorrow?"

"I cannot counsel you in this matter, but you have the right idea. Go home, figure out what you think the best words are to address the Chief. I am sure you will know what to say. You are a wise young man."

Immediately the boy went to his father's grain to fetched out a handful of millet seeds, to take along when he went to see the Chief the next day. Going off to a quiet place, he rehearsed his plan in detail, making sure to rule out any mistakes he may make when coming before the Chief.

Early the next day the boy raced down to the court, to wait for the Chief. When summonsed, he was asked to give his answer, the boy gave the handful of millet seeds to the Chief. The Chief looking at the seeds, asked the boy what he meant by this.

"What are these seeds for?"

"I want you to plant that millet, so I will have plants for my chicken when it hatches tomorrow?"

"What do you mean by this? Explain yourself."

"Sir, I am but a boy, making me unfamiliar in matters of court. Hence my answer to you O wise Chief sir, may surprise you, sounding disrespectful. I, therefore, beg you to forgive me my lack of learning."

"I understand, very well you may proceed."

"My answer to your riddle sir, is, you plant those millet seeds I gave you, so I can feed my chicken with the plants you get tomorrow when my egg hatches."

To say the Chief was a little angry would be a gross understatement. Before he addressed the boy again, he looked down at the seeds in his hand, then back at the boy, then back down at the seeds once more. Then he roared out his indignation.

"Whose words are those? Whose millet is this? Who gave you that riddle?"

"That riddle is my own sir, those millet seeds are from my father's storehouse, he gave them to me."

"I think you are lying, that is why I want to know how you came by this riddle."

This last statement by the Chief actually terrified the poor boy, but as he knew he was being honest, that is all he could come up with.

"I thought it out for myself sir, I never got the riddle from anyone, also no-one gave me those words."

The Chief recognised the words as those of his wife.

"Aaa. Who told you to 'think it out for yourself?' If I find, you have lied to me I will punish your whole family, beginning with you."

"Your wise wife sir, your wife Ziah, she knew the sheep was mine, so she was trying to help, showing me how to 'think it out for myself'. And I did. She never gave me the riddle, that is mine, Sir. I..."

That was it, the boy ran out of the court.

"She was not too wise this time."

The Chief mumbled to himself, then called for his advisors to assist in his decision against Ziah. A lengthy discussion ensued between him together with these counsellors, till a consensus was arrived at. Finally, when a verdict of guilty was reached, the Chief dismissed his advisors, summoning for Ziah to be called before him.

ZIAH'S JUDGEMENT

WHEN SHE ARRIVED, THE Chief could hardly hide his anger, calling back his advisors.

"You, of all people, being wise, should know never to interfere with decisions of state. Besides, you also know the rule I made concerning this matter to which you agreed. Because you have broken this my only rule, I have no choice, but to banish you from my court, even though you own half of all that I have. I am sending you back to your father's house."

Ziah was most indignant at her unjust treatment. Being found guilty without a fair or just defence.

"O wise Chief, may I not speak in my own defence, here before you, as well as in the presence of these your counsellors, before you sentence me?"

"The decision was made by me with my advisors before I summonsed you here. Rather, it was not a wise decision in my anger. Please, speak your defence, we are listening."

"Pray, tell me. What is the wrong I am accused of, including the circumstances thereof?"

"You are accused of counselling the young boy with the egg, who was here about his sheep. In your counsel, you gave him the answer to the riddle I set for him."

"That is not true. I taught the boy to figure things out for himself when he faces problems, which is, in fact, a skill. I did not counsel him on his case, which is set before you, because of my promise. In teaching the boy to think for himself, I did not break my promise to you, my wise Chief. The boy thought the solution out for himself, becoming the wiser for it."

"How did he get the riddle *vis-à-vis* the millet seed, if it was not from you?"

"I do not know how the boy formulated his riddle. I was not present. I simply told him to go home to figure out the riddle for himself, then present it to you this morning. Because of the oath I gave you, I could not advise him."

"Tomorrow, I will summon the boy back to hear his version more clearly. If I, with my advisors, decide you are right, then I will fetch you back when I am ready. In the meantime, because I believe you advised the boy, what I have said I have said. On this account, you are banished from my court till further notice."

"Before you dismiss me, may I ask you a question?"

"Say on."

"May I make for you one final meal before I leave and carry with me what was mine when I married you?"

"You must see that you are gone before nightfall! And you may carry whatever you need, plus cook whatever you want."

The moment Ziah arrived at home, she sent word to her father's house, to come quickly to her aid, bringing two strong men with him. During morning court, before the Chief arrived home, Ziah went to work on the Chief's favourite meal, which she served with a sumptuous amount of strong palm wine. While the servants were serving up the dessert course, the Chief fell soundly asleep in his chair. Just then, her father with the servants arrived to help her complete her plans.

THE CHIEF'S ABDUCTION

ZIAH'S FATHER HELPING the servants, loaded the Chief onto a litter to carry him back to their house. There they gave the Chief a comfortable bed. Agreeable enough for him to sleep soundly through the night.

In the morning on waking, the Chief, seeing his strange surroundings, roared his surprise in anger, rousing the whole house.

"What have you done with my house? Where am I? What am I doing here? Someone has stolen me away."

While the Chief was roaring away, he saw Ziah enter the room beaming at him.

"What have you done, you crafty woman, where am I? Oh, my head, please answer me softly, I feel like my head has been pierced through with needles."

"You are at my father's house O Chief. You instructed me to leave your house then go to my father's house. And you also said I could carry whatever I needed. I needed you, so I took you."

"You are undoubtedly an exceptionally sagacious woman. I have wronged you, including that young man, have I not?"

"Yes, you have. The answer he gave you was his own."

"I resolved all the rest of the day to tell you after dinner how I worked out what happened. Unfortunately, I was plied with a highly alcoholic mix of palm wine, consequently, this is where I am as the result. Before we go on, I must thank you for helping me with a case I was not handling well. I apologise. Will you return with me to our own home, to become my new counsellor on all matters hard to solve, for only a fool would send away such a wise woman.

"I accept. And you O wise Chief, are most assuredly no fool."

The moral of the story, you say? Always keep your temper under control, because when you lose it, you lose the argument as well.

CHAPTER 15

THE MOUSE AND THE LION

Long, long, ago somewhere in Africa, when all the people and animals were new. Lion, King of the beasts, was fast asleep on his lookout rock, having eaten a belly-swelling feast. While sleeping, perchance dreaming of plains full of wild antelope, he snored away. Well, we all can dream, right?

A small Mouse who had admired our Lion for many long days and nights decided this was the moment he could check out our King of the beasts more closely, so to speak.

Quite stealthily, on tip-toe, Mouse crept up Lion's fluffy big mane, passing dangerously close to his ear. Without regard to Lion's non-stop twitching in his sleep, he persisted in a detailed inspection of his face, whiskers and all. Finishing off there, our intrepid Mouse fearlessly continued on down to his tail.

The running down Lion's spine is what did it. Lion abruptly woke up, spinning his head around, he caught a glimpse of a Mouse sliding down his tail onto his right back paw. Instinctively Lion swiped, hooking Mouse in-between two right front paw pads.

Slowly he brought the squirming, wriggling Mouse up to his nose. Sniffing him, his tummy grumbled as he mumbled to himself.

"Hum, small but good smelling, good enough to eat as an after-dinner morsel."

Mouse was terrified, squeaking out pleas of help.

"Please sir, you are the great big fearless warrior of our forests and plains, please do not eat me, I meant you no harm. I was admiring your greatness from close up. That is it, I live with my family just outside your big den. We clean up around here, keeping your place tidy for you."

"Which is not enough reason to stop me from eating you, there are many more where you come from. Why then should I spare your life?"

"I have always looked up to you as a just king, not a murderer. I am sure you could do with a friend who will help you in times of need. You never know what the future holds for you. Also, please remember, I never hurt you in any way."

That cracked Lion up, rolling over his belly quivering with laughter. So hard did he laugh, he dropped Mouse, who wasted no time in getting out of Lion's way. Running home for all he was worth, diving into his hole, down he went, into his shelter under the big rock, safe once again. Phew!

MOUSE BACK IN TROUBLE

THE NEXT TIME MOUSE went out to look for food, Lion was waiting for him. Mouse, however, was oblivious of him hiding behind a nearby bush, then with one swipe of his paw, he had Mouse once again.

"Thought you could escape the old Lion, did you? What can you say this time, now that I have caught you fair and square?"

"You are surely the best of the best. This is why all the animals call you King of the beasts, but do you have the wisdom to go with your brawn? How do you know you will definitely never need my help someday?"

"You tiny little runt, what could you ever do for me, which I could not do for myself?"

Lion's remark came with a chuckle, as he once more sniffed Mouse with lip-smacking fondness.

"Indeed, how will you know if you have wisdom if you do not test yourself? Maybe I can help in ways you could not even think of. But this, you will never find out if you eat me."

WISDOM OF MOUSE

SOMEHOW, THIS LITTLE Mouse's reasoning was getting to Lions senses, hitting his feelings where they hurt.

"Well, you may have something in what you say. And you sure are not much of a meal in any case. So, I will test myself while also giving you a chance to prove if you are truly wise or not. Then, we will see if you are a little mouse with a big mouth or a little mouse with great wisdom."

With that, Lion let Mouse go free. But unbeknownst to Lion, he would not have to wait long before he would test the wisdom of Mouse. Besides, this would take place in a way he could never have guessed, just as Mouse had told him.

Not too many moons later, Lion on his way back to his den after an unsuccessful hunt, was brooding and grouching to himself under his breath, as he made his way down the pathway back home. When, in an instant, he found himself launched into the treetops, up into the night sky. He had been thwarted, walking right into a hanging net trap set by some hunters that day. Indignantly caught in a basket of ropes, Lion roared his head off in rage. Mostly, angry with himself for not noticing the hidden snare. From his lofty cramped position, he struggled to look around at his situation. Tightly bundled up, he slowly came to the conclusion, he was thoroughly caught, in the rope thing he was in.

Wondering if he could wriggle out, or part the ropes, he pushed and bit with every ounce of his might, but to no avail, simply adding an aching jaw to his woes. He was truly stuck. Contemplating his dire situation, considering the possibility of this being his last day. He thought of calling someone to help him in his plight. It was then he realised something, who on earth would come to a lion's aid? When out of nowhere, the words of Mouse came back to him.

"Mouse, yes, of course, Mouse. I am not far from my den."

Muttering this to himself, he remembered Mouse had told him where he stayed.

REMEMBER MOUSE

HE DECIDED A FEW LOUD roars would surely wake Mouse. He was not too worried about the hunters, for they would not come till dawn.

Lion was also well aware men never ventured into the bush at night for fear of him and his friends. So, with total confidence Lion's roars grew in volume, hoping against hopes, Mouse would hear.

Not more than a few owl hoots later, there arrived Mouse with a happy smile on his face when he saw Lion's predicament. Pleased at what he saw, he realised he could finally show Lion some of his wisdom in action after all.

"Where are the helpers, I thought you would bring helpers?"

"I first came to see what was wrong and show you I had heard you, but I can see I will be able to get you out on my own."

"Now, that is not funny. As I told you the other day, what can you, such a little chap, ever do to get me out of situations like this on your own?"

"Watch, wait and learn."

Mouse was a little annoyed at always being belittled by Lion, so he never warned him how hard he would hit the ground. He would let him figure it out for himself. Mouse could see where the trap was tied to a nearby tree, setting to work. He chewed and chewed, now and again spitting out pieces, as he worked his way through the tough fibrous rope with his strong, sharp front teeth. Gnawing with passion as he did, it was only a few nightjar calls later before he was done. Down came Lion, without warning, smartly tail spinning into the ground, landing squarely on his posterior. He let out such a loud roar, it scared some feathers off of owl as he made his fast getaway through many branches.

OUT OF A MESS AND INTO A TANGLE

EVEN AFTER LANDING on the ground, Lion was still unable to make his way out of that tangled bundle of rope he was in. Turning to look for Mouse, who by this time, was nowhere to be seen, Lion called out for his rescuer. Mouse answered from the top of a leadwood tree, eyes wide open, peering down at Lion in the middle of the clearing.

"I am fine. I am resting up here till you go home."

"No, come down I will never harm you, or call you small and useless again, as long as I live. You have shown me your wisdom, which saved my life. To hurt you would be a terribly unwise thing to do. From this night on, you will be known as my wise friend. But you need to do one more small thing for me, that is to chew off the knot to open up this tangle I am still in."

A mighty happy Mouse came down out of the leadwood tree to chew the rope for Lion, in his final step to freedom. Not long after, Mouse liberated Lion. Free again and on his feet, Lion invited Mouse to join him on his walk back home for his safety. Delighted, he accompanied the King of the beasts on his walk back home. Mouse was sure Lion was limping a little, from his prompt descent into the ground, but in a few days, he was speeding around the plains after a potential meal again.

The moral of the story, you say? When a job calls for wisdom, size and strength alone are of little use.

CHAPTER 16

WHY CHEETAH'S CHEEKS ARE STAINED

Long, long, ago somewhere in Africa, when all the people and animals were new. There lived a wicked, worthless, lazy hunter.

This hunter, from time to time and only when forced by hunger, would take up his spear to seek out food. This slothful man, as was his usual custom, sat in the shade of a tree on the top of a small kopje. Sighing with discontent, he watched plump antelope grazing on the plains below. He bemoaned his fate for having to be a hunter in the first place, with the need to hunt for food. Why could he not get meat without such tiresome work? His habit was to steal meat from some poor unsuspecting animal who had done all the work. On one hot and sultry day, he scanned the plain below, hoping to find a recent kill to steal from. This was how the lazy slob lived.

As wrong as his methods were, you may not believe that they bettered the diabolical actions of his next endeavour. Stealing meat from those innocent victims paled in comparison to that malefactor's next move. Unfortunately, this day there was no fresh kill to rob. Still occupied with his usual irritated thoughts, he kept up his searching. When unexpectedly, his eye was caught by a movement in the long grass close to an antelope herd. Suddenly, the grass exploded into life. It was a cheetah springing out, moving with the speed of the wind across the plain, then bringing down a plump buck who had unwisely strayed off from the main group. The other startled animals scattered, while the cheetah quickly dispatched with its victim.

Just as his nasty practice was, the evil hunter saw his chance to rob some meat from an innocent animal once again. Waiting a moment for the cheetah to make good its kill before going in for his meat. Still watching from the kopje, he saw the cheetah drag her quarry to some nearby trees where three fine-looking cheetah cubs appeared. These were obediently hiding in wait while their mother to make her kill.

It was then our good-for-nothing's whole being was filled with jealousy when he saw this scene. If only he could eat fresh meat like these cheetah cubs every day, without having to hunt or scrounge for it. With these thoughts swirling through his head, he swiftly came up with his malicious plan. Tired of always eating un-fresh meat, he decided he wanted to eat freshly caught met the way those cubs did. It was then he schemed a horrible plan.

This lazy degenerate concocted the idea to steal a cheetah cub, thinking to train it to hunt for him. As the shadows grew longer while the sun began to sink, the cheetah hid her cubs under some bushes with the meat, going off to the river for a drink. This was his chance, so quickly he grabbed his spear, scurrying down the kopje to the bushes where he saw the cubs being concealed. Too young to be afraid of him, the cubs lay still while he dithered, trying to pick the best one to steal. Unable to make up his mind, he took all three of the cubs, thinking three cheetahs to hunt for him, would undoubtedly be better than one.

The mother cheetah returned from the waterhole to find her cubs gone. Although she searched the bushes in the surrounding grass, plaintively calling for them the whole time, there was no sign of her babies anywhere. Broken-hearted and desolate, she kept on searching while she cried and cried. How long she cried, no one knows, but with her incessant weeping, as the days went by, her tears made dark stains down her cheeks.

As she cried, the sound of her sobbing was heard by an old prophet passing through the wilderness. Wanting to know the reason for this cheetah's misery, he decided to investigate. Troubled by her strange behaviour, he took a closer look. He noticed she was relentlessly searching roundabout one group of bushes calling and crying as she went. Then from the signs, he observed on the ground, he saw the cheetah was concentrating under one bush in particular. It was there he spotted she had last hidden her cubs.

GOOD COUNSEL NEEDED

THIS OLD PROPHET WAS well known to be wise and knowledgeable in the ways of the wild. And he was also known for his care for the animals. After he saw the signs, he was convinced the cheetah was searching for lost cubs. But what caused them to go missing in the first place?

While the prophet combed the grass throughout the surrounding area, looking for clues of what had happened to the cheetah's babies, he had a thought. He was mystified by the reason for the missing cubs. Then he noticed all the tracks had been wiped clean around the bushes, which made the old prophet suspicious. As a result of this, he decided to go to the people of the local village, to make enquiries.

After going through the village asking questions, he learned from the people regarding the wicked hunter and what he had done, which made him very angry. The hunter, on top of being lazy and worthless, was also a wretched thief breaking the traditions of the people. It was common knowledge that hunters were to use their own strength and skills for hunting. This man's ways would surely bring dishonour to the whole tribe, including all who hunted for their food.

When the old prophet told the elders of the village, what had happened to the cheetah. They gathered a group of men together with strict instructions to find, bind and then remove the wicked man from their midst. Then they were to take him beyond the mountains into the desert, leaving him there to learn how to fend for himself. The elected men did as they were told, first binding the lazy reprobate, then doing to him as the elders had instructed them. Abandoning him deep in the desert, where they left him to fend for himself. In the meantime, the old prophet took the three cheetah cubs, returning them back to their grateful mother.

But the long weeping and sobbing of the mother cheetah had stained her face forever. So, you will see, even today, the tear-stains on a cheetah's face are there to remind all hunters, it is not honourable or noble to hunt without the traditional respect that must be given to all animals.

From that day to this, many honourable tribes and peoples, have the custom of dressing up in their proudest apparel when they go out on a hunt. This is done as a mark of respect to the animals, as well as gratitude to their creator.

The moral of the story, you say? A life is a life, no matter what the life and the virtuous actions of a righteous man repairs the breach.

CHAPTER 17

HYENA, LION AND SQUIRREL

Long, long, ago somewhere in Africa, when all the people and animals were new. One crispy spring morning, Hyena wakened from a deep sleep, yawned a few times, then stretched his wiry old frame into shape, preparing himself for the hunt.

The old fellow, now alone in his mature years, decided on the valley for an easy hunt, moseyed on down the pathway. Deep in thought, passing by a pile of old bones, his belly grumbled from the memory of a one-time tasty meal.

Right there, in the vicinity of the old bones, he began to sniffle around for more of the same, hoping to chance upon a rabbit – or maybe two – that may show themselves for a tasty morsel. In this way, nose to the ground he continued on his way down to the valley, ever hopeful.

All the while, Squirrel, of the arboreal – tree – species was cautiously watching. As Hyena passed on by below him, muttered to himself.

"I do not trust that Hyena. Not one little bit."

This, of course, was not without good cause, knowing Hyena would eat him in a trice, given the first opportunity, but Hyena was paying him no mind. All the same, Squirrel was keeping a close watch, hopping from tree to tree as Hyena inspected the terrain piece by piece on his ramble through the damp grass.

If Squirrel were to think he had gone unnoticed by the old loner, he would be highly mistaken. Hyena never got to be so old and fit, without all his wits being well-honed by age and experience.

AN OLD WARRIOR GIVES A LESSON

SPEAKING OF WITS, HYENA noticed a young heavy-maned lion exercising his right to hunt in the same valley. It did not take him long to recognise this newcomer was actually hunting him!

"Oh, oh!"

Coming up with a quick plan, he slowly and purposefully made his way back to the pile of bones, the ones he passed earlier on his way down to the valley.

You know the ones? The bones which made his tummy grumble? Yes, those bones, he was making his way back to those old bones, while the lion stalked him ever closer, slinking from bush to bush intently eyeing him as he went. Hyena, in the meantime, settled down next to his old friends to wait things out.

The lion in position and seeing a chance to pounce, manoeuvred himself into a good position, tucking his paws tightly under his belly, ready for the right moment.

You will surely know that lions and hyenas are lifelong, mortal enemies, so this is no strange situation for either beast to be in.

Well, continuing with the story, we have Hyena lying down chewing on one of the more tasty-looking bones. Crunching away, then perceiving the lion was about to spring, he loudly exclaimed.

"Man, that was one delicious lion! I wonder if there are more around here? I am starving,"

Standing up to look around, he burped, licking his chops.

Lion, meanwhile ceasing any springing plans, slinked away backwards, creeping behind every bush he could find in his retreat. Eventually, out of danger's way, he stood up, shaking the dust from his mane while he chided himself.

"Wow, that was close. I nearly turned myself into a hyena's breakfast! Imagine that!"

WISDOM WILL ALWAYS HAVE ITS DAY

IT WILL COME AS NO surprise to you, that Squirrel was watching this whole affair from his lofty arboreal – tree – position. Following Lion and perching himself high above him in a tall tree, to avoid turning himself into a snack, he announced his presence.

"Ahoy there! Ahum Lion! It is me, Squirrel, your friend for the future."

Lion looked up, squinting into the sunlight, there he saw Squirrel sporting a silly grin peering down at him. Realising Squirrel probably saw the whole scene, he embarrassingly cleared his throat.

"Ahem, ahem, what do you want?"

"It is not what I want, that is in question. It is what you want from me, which matters."

Lion was curious at Squirrel's odd remark.

"And what might that be?"

"Well, being a wise lion and all, I am sure you know, I saw the drama unfold between you and that sneaky hyena."

"I did. But why a sneaky hyena?"

Lion's obvious curiosity brought Squirrel down a peg or two closer. Squirrel, as you can imagine, spilt the beans, telling Lion about the trick Hyena played on him. Lion was furious, jumping up – because he had lain down again – inviting Squirrel to climb on his back for a ride to where he last left Hyena.

While riding on Lions back, Squirrel reckoned things should have been like this from the beginning. Naturally, you can understand Squirrel's intentions were noble! In aid of bettering his own position in life, plus having the opportunity to come out big with Lion. Squirrel, for good reason, thought all would be trumps for him and his kind throughout the whole district. After all, we squirrels must stand together in a common cause against every sneaky hyena.

Hyena meanwhile was lying quietly gazing at that old pile of bones, well pleased with himself for foxing Lion. Suddenly, off in the distance, he saw the two gallant adventurers coming his way. Lion was doing the quickstep, striding out as bold as brass with a look to kill. Hyena knew without a doubt, this called for further wise action if he was to save his hide yet again.

Quickly formulating his plan, Hyena was ready for them. Nonchalantly, turning his attention back to his bones, he deliberately faced away from the oncoming lion. In this way he waited patiently, pretending not to have seen the two, till they were almost on top of him, before shouting out.

"Where is that lazy squirrel? I am ravenous! It has been ages since I sent him to bring me another lion!"

Hyena's belly ached with laughter, as he watched a streaking lion make his way back up the valley. As for Squirrel, Hyena searched high and low, but he has never been seen since. Must have left the district.

The moral of the story, you say? Age and skill will always overcome youth and treachery!

CHAPTER 18

THE KIND-HEARTED HUNTER

Long, long, ago somewhere in Africa, when all the people and animals were new. There was a tiny village on the edge of the jungle. Not too far outside this village lived a widow woman together with her teenage son. The woman's husband had been a hunter, who was killed by a rogue elephant while setting his traps for food in the jungle.

Bereft of her husband she was forced to work full days, even into the night, to get enough food for herself and her young boy. But even with her hard work, they lived poorly and mostly half-starved.

The reason for this came from the boy being an only child. After her husband died in such a violent way, the boy's mother was overly protective of him. Therefore, it stood to reason she did not want her son to be a hunter. The young lad, named Tau by his father, was the nineteenth – Tau - generation from his tribe's settlement in Africa. Even though old enough to hunt and having been taught by his father to set traps or hunt with bow and arrow, it did not sway Tau's mother enough to let him add to the food coffers as a hunter.

Instead, Tau's chores were set by his mother, which involved helping around the house, tending the small crop patch, including gathering wild roots. Also, aiding her with her crafts and going to the village from time to time to sell their wares. The money they made was only enough to buy meagre supplies of staples, with which to feed themselves. The young man, however, was becoming unhappy with the way they lived.

"Mother, we are always hungry. Please let me go out to set some traps. I am sure we will do better than we are now. If I do not take care of you, my mother, I am worse than an infidel. Do not let me be as one unable to take care of his own mother."

"My dear son, you help me every day, how could you be as an infidel. You are precious to me and you are my only family. I am afraid for your life. Besides, what will I do alone, if you are killed by some wild beast as your father was?"

"You have the home father built and your handy work is good, but it is enough to feed you only. I see how you go hungry for my sake. But I cannot keep seeing you go hungry anymore. I must go hunting for your sake. I will only set traps at the edge of the jungle, where it is safe. I promise not to go bow hunting without discussing it with you first, or if you decide to let me. But Mother, eat we must."

Sitting under the stars in half moonlight around the fire, their discussion went on late into the night. A little after midnight, when the moon went down in the western sky, Tau's mother relented.

AND A HUNTER IS BORN

THE NEXT DAY, BEFORE the sun gave its full light, a happy young hunter carrying his axe and spear, sling, bow and arrows slung over his shoulders for protection, left to work in the jungle. Day one, he spent cutting branches till the sun began to give up its light before he made his way back home.

The day following, he left before the sun was fully above the horizon because the work was much and their supplies were dangerously low. Cleverly, he rearranged the branches till they formed traps as he observed his father do, labouring on till another day was spent.

Into his third day, Tau needed strong ropes. Remembering how his father would strip bark from a special tree, he did the same. Cleaning, stripping, wetting while shaping, till he wove enough thick, strong ropes ready for his traps.

A week into his work, he completed several traps, setting them up in the pathways the animals used. He disguised them so well, not even a human walking by would see them. By the week's end, he completed the necessary traps he thought he would need.

Once the traps were set, all he could do was wait. Inspecting them daily, careful to remember where they were, memorising them off by heart. This way, Tau made sure he would not be caught in one of his own traps.

After three days of waiting, he received his reward, with two traps sprung containing a buck in each. The following day there were three traps sprung, with an animal in each one of them. The grazing was good, bringing a plentiful supply of game. This success caused Tau to prepare his bountiful catches for market. When they were ready, he set off into town selling his stock of salted skins and meat without any trouble. With the proceeds from his sale, the young hunter bought grain, including much-needed supplies for the home. He bought fine salt, millet, sorghum, vinegar, together with coarse salt for drying meat and skins. In addition, he bought extra spices for preserving the dried meat. Included in his supplies, he bought herbs for what they cooked, some for the pot, some for the meat to be cooked on the open fire.

Things were changing, making life good for Tau and his mother. They were finally both getting enough food at last. Tau felt proud of his accomplishments, noticing their situation, he believed he could no longer be called an infidel. Tau's mother was obviously extremely proud of her son's achievements. She was also able to increase her trinkets for sale because of her son's many supplies.

Their good fortune continued while the rains came, bringing abundant food for the game to eat, allowing them to live comfortably for the first time since the death of husband and father. But as the season moved on the rains stopped, the grazing withered, then with it went the plentiful supply of game. As a result, the traps caught less and less game the further they progressed into the winter months. Regardless of Tau's efforts in skillfully shifting his traps regularly in hopeful expectation, he received no reward.

One night, much like the one when Tau convinced his mother to let him set up traps in the first place, they spoke again. This time he needed his mother's permission to go further into the jungle to try there with his traps for a better chance of success. The young man's mother had been anticipating such a day, for some time already.

Without a murmur, she gave her consent, having witnessed how Tau's father had surely taught him well, for the results were proof enough. Persuaded her boy had become a hunter.

DEEPER INTO THE JUNGLE

A SHORT WHILE AFTER he moved his traps further into the jungle, the young hunter caught a sizable monkey. As he approached the trap, his spear in hand at the ready to strike, the monkey spoke.

"Son of Adam, you are but a youth. If you kill me, you will be doing what all men seem to do, which is evil."

"What might that be?"

"All of mankind are vile killers, killing just for the sake of killing, without so much as a moment's consideration for the animal he is about to kill. That is, does it, that is me, have a family with children to care for or not? What do they care, it is in the trap, just kill it anyway? Which is how they killed my brother and his family. Are you like this? Because if you are, make it quick, so I do not screech, thereby frightening my youngsters. But if you are not, you could let me go, you never know, I may one day help you, if you are ever in need. In this way, we will become friends."

The youth was moved by what the monkey said, besides, he did not eat monkeys. Anyway, he liked the idea of knowing one as a friend, letting him out of the trap. Once out, the monkey jumped up onto the branch of a nearby tree.

"You are a rare creature, young man."

"Why is that Monkey?"

"I see you have a good heart, which is both good and bad. Be wise whom you help. Remember, by no means do a good turn for a man, because they are all bad, always paying back harm for good. But I will remember you, my friend."

With that, Monkey ran off to join his family. The next day Tau found a hefty snake in another of his traps. The moment he saw it, he turned to seek help from the villagers, but the snake shouted after him. The snake perceived where the youth was headed.

"Stop son of Adam. There is no need to call the villagers to come to kill me. I will do you no harm. Although I pray, let me out of this intricately made trap of yours. I am impressed, for no matter how hard I tried to get out, my efforts were in vain. I do not suppose you eat snake, do you?"

"No, I have never eaten a snake. I hope under no circumstance to do so either."

"Well then, it would do you no harm to let me out of here. For you cannot know what may lie in your future. Maybe one day I will be able to do you a good turn for sparing my life. Also, I in no way forget a good deed done for me."

Tau would not deny he was afraid of the massive snake, but taking him at his word, he opened the trap, letting him out. When the snake was out, he turned to the youth.

"Young man you are unlike the rest of mankind, who is cruel, with evil intent. I see you have a tender spirit. A word of wisdom I leave you for letting me out. In nowise trust man, you will be sorely disappointed if you ever help one out."

Snake slithered off, leaving the young hunter to continue resetting his trap. Before returning home, he went on to check his other traps, finding them empty.

Early the next day Tau was back, checking his traps as usual. This day he found a hare which was killed by the design of one of his little traps. Tau's father taught him to respect all animals, never to let them suffer. This is why he taught Tau to set traps, which instantly killed the smaller creatures the moment they set them off. As for the bigger traps, they cleverly scooped up their prey, which merely hung in the net unharmed, till the hunter came along to make his decision.

Today Tau, who had been getting quite weak from the lack of food went joyfully back home early, to prepare for dinner. After a long drought, he and his mother were finally blessed with fresh food to eat.

On the following day, our young hunter found a large black-maned lion in his one trap. Keeping a long distance away from this trap, he stood there planning his next move, when the lion smelling his presence turned to look at him. The lion noticing the youth's apprehension, speaking kindly to him, albeit in a loud voice though.

"Son of Adam, you need not be afraid of me, an old lion with almost blunt teeth. Come near that I may reason with you. I hate shouting."

The young hunter gingerly approached the trap till he was five paces away.

"You, young man, are a skilful hunter. I have not ever been caught in one of these contraptions before. Although I have heard accounts of them from others of the animal kingdom. I have always been able to see them before I got too close, but your trap I was not even able to catch a glimpse of, till I found myself indignantly bundled up skywards. Congratulations, now could you please let me out? I am sure you do not eat lion, or do you?"

"No, I could not eat a lion, in any case, you are much too old and tough. What concerns me, is you eating me!"

"Ho, ho, ho, that is funny. Firstly, I am not a man-eater, nor do I intend to be. Man disgusts me, because of how he behaves towards us animals, as well to one another. I avoid man at all times. But you seem to be different. Now, as to my release? Are you or are you not going to let me out of this confounded trap of yours? I am getting cramps."

The youth hesitated to move closer, which Lion noticed.

"Son of Adam, there is no reason to be afraid, I will most certainly never harm you. In fact, I will be indebted to you for saving my life. Therefore I will be ready to aid you, should you ever be in need of my help in this here forest of mine."

Taking Lion at his word, the youth released the trap setting him free again.

"Thank you, but before I leave, remember what I said about man, it is a no-good thing to trust him if you value your safety. And thank you for setting me free."

So, Lion proudly and regally made his way back along the game path once again, slowly melting back into the vast jungle, home once again, as it should be.

Of the strangest things to happen to the young hunter, was to find a man trapped in one of his snares some weeks later.

The man was extremely angry with the youth, shouting all kinds of abuse the moment he set eyes on him. Tau listened, although he said nothing, remembering the words of Monkey, Snake, then lastly, Lion only weeks ago. Therefore, he offered the man an apology by way of explanation.

"Sir, I am a poor hunter, as was my father, till he was killed by a rogue elephant while setting up one of his snares deeper into the jungle. My mother and I are poor, having lost our only provider. For this reason, the responsibility has fallen on me to feed us both. If that is an evil thing, then I am unable to answer you for all the abuse you are laying on me."

"I am not interested in your troubles, they cannot be worse than mine. I have been in this miserable thing of yours all night. I demand you let me out at once."

Tau let the irate bad man out without a word. Once out, the man thought it wise to resist attacking a strong youth, as well-armed as the young hunter was. Turning his back without even a thank you, he left in a different direction from which Tau came.

A SEASON OF CHANGE

THE SEASON WAS DICTATING to Tau, that change was necessary. His traps were no longer catching the game he needed for the two of them to survive.

"Mother, it will be full moon soon, in which case, this is the best time for me to travel."

The gentle mother once again knew the imminent time for Tau's departure deeper into the forest was coming. She had seen it many times before with his father.

"My dear son, I have made plans for your departure for some days already. Saving you millet for cakes, to be eaten with the salted, dried meat you prepared for this coming winter. These you will need for your journey. When will you be leaving, so I can bake the cakes and pack for you?"

"In two days. But Mother, I can hunt for small creatures on the way to feed myself. If you give me from our little rations, what will you eat?"

"I am fine, I too have resources in my trinkets I sell. While you have been bringing in the food, I have been stocking up for sale through the winter. Knowing the day would come when you would leave for the jungle. For this, my prayers go with you, my son."

Many things were talked about under the moonlit night. And Tau heard many tales of how his father went about his trade when winter was upon them. That night he learned vital information from his mother to help him on his new journey.

On the day of his departure, he filled his small bag with coarse salt, spices, a fire flint, wood shavings, his dried meat and the cakes his mother baked. This bag he flung over his left shoulder. Wrapped around his waist, he wore a kaross his father made from a kudu skin. Spear in hand, sling, bow and arrows over his other shoulder plus a waterskin around his neck, he bid his precious mother goodbye before walking away. Reminding her not to worry, because as soon as he had food to bring home, he would be back.

Leaving early, he made good time to the inner jungle, as he could tell from the position of the sun. Something Tau's father failed to teach him, was how to find his way around in unfamiliar terrain, consequently, before long he realised he was lost. Failing to remember his way home, he resolved to continue hunting for food, before worrying about his way home. He would cross that bridge when he killed something to eat, which in his estimation, should be soon.

Lost, for two weeks without a proper meal including two days without water, unsuccessful in his hunting endeavours, Tau's energy was spent. He could find no water in his wanderings through the jungle. Pulling off the kaross from his waist, he laid it on the ground in the shade of a big tree, then he lay down to escape the burning sun, which was making him more thirsty. Worsening his situation, he was suffering from dehydration.

As he lay there looking up into the tree, his mind wandered over the plans he made, realising how so many things had gone wrong for him. He kept shaking his head to clear his fuzzy feeling. He began to despair of his lot in life, wondering about his mother, how would she manage, having her only surviving relative also die in the jungle? Would this force her to leave the district? This, along with many other things, crossed his confused mind, while going in and out of consciousness. A host of questions, like why, was he inept at finding his way around? Still, deep in thought, a piece of bark landed on his chest from somewhere above him. He stared into the deep green shady cover above him, hoping it was not a leopard. Then he saw it, a monkey landing on a branch high above him. That must have done it.

Tau gazed up at the noisy monkey, but he was incapable of hearing what it was chattering about, as it swung its way down in his direction. Once on the ground, standing next to the youth still staring bewilderedly, the monkey repeated its questions.

"Where have you come from son of Adam and where are you going? Even more, why are you lying here under my tree as if one dying?"

The young hunter heard only some of what Monkey was saying above the high-pitched singing in his ears. A strange look of doubt came over Monkeys face, still staring at the young man.

"Is it you son of Adam, who saved my life from your trap?"

"Yes, it is me."

"You do not look good, young man."

"Oh Monkey, it is good to see you. I am lost without food or water. When I could not go any further, I lay down here to die, because my strength has left me. Berries and some roots I have eaten, but water I have been unable to find."

"I will be back in a moment."

Monkey grabbed the youths waterskin lying next to him, running off through the bush. In no time, he was back with the bag filled.

"Here drink, it is good, but only a little. First, you must eat. I will be back shortly."

Monkey went off again to fetch wild soft fruits, besides this, he remembered some raw honey he left in a tree hole where he last raided a beehive.

When the youth had eaten, Monkey asked him again where he was headed. Tau told him how he needed food for himself and his mother through winter. It was while out hunting when he became lost somewhere around twenty days ago.

"You still need to hunt, you will not be able to go back home yet. You first need to build up your strength. Come I will show you the water fountain in the rocks as well as where you can hunt. When you are ready, you come back here, this is my tree where I live, the family is out gathering food, but they will be back before sundown."

Once fed, and his immediate thirst taken care of, Tau went to Monkey's fountain where he filled his leather bag. Feeling somewhat revived, he set off to hunt where Monkey showed him. Before Monkey left Tau, he pointed him the way back to his tree when he should be ready to return.

LOST IN THE JUNGLE ONCE MORE

TWO DAYS LATER UNSUCCESSFUL with his hunt Tau was lost again. Aimlessly ambling about he could not find Monkey's tree or the fountain. All places looked so alike to him. Then out of nowhere, a loud voice sounded right behind him.

"Where are you going son of Adam?"

It was Lion who quietly following the young hunter as he wandered, first in one direction, then in the other, as a drunken one.

"You scared me almost out of my skin, Lion."

"My turn to catch you. It is good to see you, but I think you are lost, by the way, you are stumbling through the bush. Do you need help, for I am fully ready to repay you for your kindness to me?"

"You are right, I am lost, nor able to find anything to hunt, in addition to being terribly hungry."

"Stay here awhile, wait for the old lion to bring you some solid food."

Presently Lion was back sooner than he or the youth expected, carrying a big mouthful of fresh meat from the kill he just made, dropping it in front of the youth.

"Take, cook and eat. This will give you strength for some time to come."

"Where did you get this animal, I have been stalking around in this jungle for weeks without finding a thing?"

"I have seen your tracks going around in big circles, scaring the game for miles in every direction. I will have to show you where to go, but for now, cook and eat your food."

Soon after his meal, the young hunter went with Lion, who led him to the Impala he killed earlier.

"Now, here is some meat, do what you do, then take what you need for your journey back home. Look, from here you can see a small hill. Head for that, when you get there, you will see the Chief's village. It is far from your village, although when you get there, they will show you your way back to your own village. I have a long way to go and my family is waiting for me."

"Farewell Lion, thank you for saving my life."

"You spared my life once and I always remember a good deed done to me. Farewell, my good friend, may we meet again someday soon, under better circumstances next time."

Lion left, with Tau cutting up the Impala using his spear. After salting the meat and skin, he loaded what he could carry to take back home for him and his mother.

Days later, lost again, having eaten all the food which Lion gave him, he was once again left with nothing to take home. The reason was, he wandered off his track for five days. This Tau felt was a good thing, since he was finally learning how to navigate in the dense bush by the position of the sun, making note of markers, such as big trees, anthills and streams. On the right path again, he managed to find the hillock Lion indicated to him. When Tau came to the hill, he wasted no time in climbing it. Once on top of its big uppermost rock, he stood up to look for the village. Without warning he was almost flown of it by a mighty eagle, with wings outstretched beyond the length of a man. After attacking him several times, forcing him flat down on his face, it finally came to rest on a branch of a rock fig tree next to him.

"What is wrong with you? You could have killed me."

"What are you looking for? Eggs?"

"Why? Do you have some?"

"No, no. Well yes. What has that to do with you?"

"Nothing, I am lost. Lion sent me here to find my way out of the jungle."

"You know Lion? You mean the old goat from the middle of the jungle? The one with the blunt teeth?"

"Yes, I know him, as I said, it was he who sent me here to locate the Chief's village from the top of this hill."

"You being a friend of Lion, changes matters. You are most welcome to be here, any friend of Lion is a friend of mine. He is a creature of wisdom, possessing kindness like few in this jungle. I am ready to be of service to anyone who Lion approves of."

Apologising humbly to Tau, he began making amends. After much talk, Eagle not only showed the young man how to find the village. But also taught him many lessons in finding his direction in ways only eagles know, even in the thickest of jungles. Eagle, after all, was a master of navigation.

"Young man I have seen you many times in the past, because you are one of the few people brave enough to venture as far into the jungle as you have, especially alone. I will be looking out for you into the future. If I see you are wondering or lost, I will be there to help."

"Thank you, Eagle, you have given me plenty of hope, at a time when my belief for getting back home was fast slipping away. I am sure we will be meeting soon again."

"Oh yes, we will meet again soon, I am certain of that. In the interim, I will be overshadowing you till you find your way out of the jungle. Go in peace son of Adam, you have a new friend."

"Farewell Eagle, I will be looking up more often from now on and thank you."

When our intrepid young hunter eventually found his way out of the jungle into the clear skies again, he waved to Eagle above him. Eagle cried goodbye, circling round he flew back home.

Though still a long way from the village, but a short distance from the forest, Tau discovered an abandoned well, looking around he found no means to draw water. Wondering if the water in the well was full enough to reach, he quickly turned back to looked down and the moment he did, his face was met by a great big snake coming up at him. Falling back from fright, he dropped his spear, but still, he scrambled further backwards on his hands and heels, his eyes ever fixed on the huge snake, approaching him.

"Son of Adam, is that you?"

The strong, but quiet voice reminded the young man, this was none other than the big snake he freed from his snare at summer's end.

"Yes, Snake, it is me."

"Why are you so far from your home?"

"I went out hunting for food, to feed my mother and myself through the winter then I became lost in the jungle. That was so many days ago, I cannot even remember how long anymore."

"Sorry for frightening you, my friend. I was coming out when you looked down. You must be thirsty if you are looking down a well. Give me your water bag, I will fill it."

Snake took the empty water bag in his mouth, then to the young hunter's surprise, he went off back in the direction of the jungle, not down the well. A short while later, he returned with a full bag, giving it to Tau.

"Why did you go toward the jungle when the well is right here?"

"Oh, that well has been empty for a long, long time. It used to be filled from the water in the jungle when it was a wishing well. But the people stopped putting in small treasures, as was the custom for centuries, so the well dried up. My forefathers have lived there since that time, which is where I now live. I have a gift for you, young man. Wait here a moment, give me the small bag you have for your food?"

Snake went off back down the well, bringing back the bag stuffed to the brim, giving it to the youth. Peering inside, young Tau could almost not believe his eyes. The little bag was full of treasures, containing silver and gold necklaces, gleaming rings, headbands, bracelets and earrings. His gratitude to snake showed no bounds. Snake, however, dismissed the young hunter's effusiveness with a chuckle, since he found no use for such things.

"What you have seen, never repeat to anyone. The knowledge of the well's treasures has been long lost in time. That is my gift to you and your mother for a storehouse to keep you both when bad times come, till you learn to hunt the jungle. I remember your kindness, even though you were so greatly afraid, you still let me go free."

When the young man drank his fill, he hung the small waterskin back around his neck again. Standing up, with his now full little bag well succoured about his waist, Tau said his farewells to Snake, who did the same.

"I will not forget you, my young friend. Go well till we meet again."

"I will always remember you, Snake. I will come to visit every time I find myself in this part of the jungle. Look after yourself. Once again thank you for your kind gift to my mother and me."

"You have more than earned it young man."

THE CHIEF'S VILLAGE

REACHING THE BIG CHIEF's village, the first one Tau came across was an old man sitting outside a house reading a manuscript of some kind who waved to him. Perceiving him to be friendly, Tau decided to approach the old man who on closer inspection looked somewhat like a sage.

"Sir, I have come on a long journey, therefore I am looking for somewhere to buy food. I humbly pray you to point me the way."

"Trouble yourself no further young man, come inside. My wife will give you food. I would not be fit to be called a man if I did not serve my fellow human beings. Albeit a travelling stranger in need, especially a youth new to his surroundings."

This old man made Tau awfully afraid with his kindness. He had never experienced such hospitality from a stranger before. Surprised and shy, he followed the old man into his home. But as he was about to go in, he noticed someone a short way off obviously staring at them. Immediately he recognised it was the bad man who was caught in his trap in the late summer.

Inside, the young hunter introduced himself to the sage and his wife. The sage's wife brought him a bowl of warm water, a washcloth, and towel to dry himself. His hosts invited him to be seated while the old lady brought out a large gourd of sour milk, including grain cakes, wild fruits and dates.

"Please do not be shy, help yourself, young man. You look like you could do with some fattening up."

"Thank you, ma'am, how right you are."

While Tau was eating, the sage reflected on the fact that his young guest was a hunter and knew hunters did not carry much money with them into the jungle. Being concerned for him, he asked the youth how he intended paying for food and lodging in the village.

"Young man I see you are a hunter. Do you have enough money for lodgings?

"Excuse me."

Tau jumped up from the table, rushing out the front door to where he left his goods outside next to the door. He looked down for his bag, but it was gone.

"I am sorry for the sudden rush, I left my bag here outside your door, now I see it is gone."

"This is strange. I leave many things at the side of my chair, like these valuable manuscripts, no one would dare take them. I wonder what this means? Do you think someone may have stolen your bag here in full daylight?"

"When you mentioned, 'if I had enough money to pay my way,' I remembered seeing a man I know, staring at us when we went inside. This made me think of my possessions out here. I would never go into a stranger's house with my hunting weapon's. Therefore, I left them out here with my bag."

"Wait here, young man I am going to the chief to inform him before the robbers get too far."

The old sage scarcely went five paces, when a group of well-armed warriors, followed by scores of people walked straight up to the little house, demanding to seize the young hunter. The bad man was standing among them, shouting for the warriors to take hold of Tau, pointing him out. Seizing Tau, they took him back to the Chief, with his hands tied behind him.

The warriors gave the Chief the young hunters little bag. Before the Chief could look into the bag, the bad man shouted a warning.

"Do not look inside because the boy is a wizard and I know he is a snake man."

While he ranted and raved, Snake quietly unnoticed by anyone, snuck up behind him lying at his feet. With a big shout, a warrior near him noticed Snake. Running backwards, he was followed by more warriors, pointing out the snake at his feet.

"You are the wizard. See the huge snake from the well is at your feet."

The bad man, when he saw the snake, was so gripped with fear, he remained frozen on the spot. The crowd shouted for the Chief to kill it.

"Be silent, I am the Chief. I make the decisions around here. Leave the snake, he will not harm anyone. Besides, he has pointed out to me who the criminal is. Young man, have you any knowledge of your accuser and is it safe for me to look into your bag?"

"Yes, I have come across this man before and yes, it is safe to open my bag."

"What is your name? How do you know this man and why is he accusing you this way?"

"My name is Tau sir. I am acquainted with him, but I am not aware of what he is accusing me of. No one has told me."

"This man has accused you of being a wizard and a thief. It is for this reason he has brought me this bag. Saying you have stolen the contents thereof by means of wizardry and that is the reason I ordered your capture. So then, it stands to reason I would like to hear your side of things."

Tau proceeded to tell the Chief his story, how the bad man was caught in one of his traps, also, how he saved him by letting him out. As for the treasures in the bag, he explained they were a gift given to him for his mother. But he could not understand any reason for the man to hate him so much, or why he would go to such lengths.

"Chief, why am I being treated as though I was a criminal, or even more, a sorcerer? I have wronged no one, I am a simple hunter going about my trade. I am on my way home to bring food to my mother, who is there alone. So why does this man tell such lies about me."

"There are many bad people in this world, young man. As a Chief, I have seen too many in my lifetime, this is but another one. As to why my son, only God knows. I will judge this man according to his deeds. He will never trouble anyone here again. Untie this young man. Tau, as the Chief, I address you in the presence of my people, I invite you to enter or go in my village, when and how you like. Here, take your bag, go in peace, young man."

"Thank you, Chief. I have made friends here and your invitation is truly welcome."

When everyone's attention was drawn to the Chief, Snake disappeared unnoticed once again.

Tau, in the meantime, received his little bag back from the Chief. Turning to the kind sage and his wife, he thanked them both for their unselfish hospitality, restoring his hope in mankind again. They insisted Tau return with them and finish his meal. When he had eaten his meal and ready to leave, he greeted them both warmly with a promise.

"I promise, whenever I pass this way on my hunting trips, I will come to visit you with a gift of meat."

"Go well, my young son. I hope you have good success with your hunting from here on. My wife and I wish you everything you wish for yourself and give greetings to your mother."

Tau finally set his face toward home and to his waiting mother. On his way, he eventually found an Impala, which he killed using his bow and arrow. After skinning the animal, he salted the meat he could carry, wrapping it inside the salted skin he prepared, leaving the rest to the animals and birds of prey. Resuming his journey, Tau proudly slung his quarry onto his shoulders. Pleased with his good fortune, he silently praised his father for the skills he so patiently taught him.

First, he went via their village to see if his mother was there. A quick search around with questions here and there, the people told him she was last seen more than a week before. The news worried Tau, till he began his ascent up the hill to their little home next to the jungle. Still some way off, with his heavy burden, he was brought up short by shouting from the top of the hill. Looking up towards the house, there, running down the pathway, was his mother coming to greet him. Stopping where he was, Tau unloaded his heavy load, dumping everything onto the side of the track. There he waited to greet his loving mother, who ran into his open arms.

Joy unspeakable filled their hearts as mother and son embraced, spinning round and round, on the dusty pathway as they laughed, and laughed.

Tau, finally home once again.

The morel of the story, you say? Your destiny rules, so never give up hope.

CHAPTER 19

HOW HIPPO LOST HIS HAIR

Long, long, ago somewhere in Africa, when all the people and animals were new. Hippo had long hair. You laugh! This is the story of how hippo lost his long hair. Hare. No, not that hair, this Hare! As I was saying, Hare became pretty tired of Hippo's vanity.

Oh yes, Hippo was once more than a little handsome indeed. That once, was due to Hippo's hairiness. In fact, hairy all over, as well as highly silky was his hair, from his head to his long fluffy tail. Well, irrefutably so. But, was it necessary to be overcome by your own beauty? No. Undeniably not. Now that is what happened to Hippo

For instance, Leopard is beautiful, so is Lion, not to mention Kudu, Bushbuck and of course Sable in his fine tuxedo, Zebra do not forget Zebra, then surely, we cannot forget Giraffe. Lanky, yes, but oh ever so graceful. So, tell me, is there anything wrong with graceful? Absolutely, not.

You see, Hare, was such a graceful creature too. It was he, that is Hare, who was most offended at Hippos' self-aggrandizement. After all, he was little, therefore he naturally blended into the veld. Well, most of the time, except when his ears stuck out. It was as a result of Hare's habits of going about feeding unnoticed in the veld, which led to Hippo being taught an everlasting lesson.

Hare, as you know, crawls and hops about in the scrub, hidden away from peering eyes, including those of Hippo, except when his ears stuck out. It was for this reason, Hare was in the-best-seat-in-the-house so as to say, when it came to the vanities of Hippo at any rate. Hare saw Hippo gazing at his image in the water's reflection nearly the entire day, except on the days it rained. He would then mumble his own praises to himself, like how he was the most handsomest animal of the whole animal kingdom.

OH, VANITY OF VANITIES

FOR AN EXAMPLE, HIPPO'S unenviable nature led him to the practice of demeaning other animals in the kingdom.

Starting with Lion, Hippo would compare his mighty mane of hair, whilst looking at his fine reflection in the waterhole.

"Lion is a wimp, aside of me. Surely, I am the king of the beasts? He looks like a shaggy dog, no match for my beauty"

Added to this, Hare heard how he mocked Leopard, as well.

"Oh Leopard. Look at me with my silky shiny fur. Not all pock marked, like your messy patch of flowers."

Hippo, barreling with laughter at his own jokes. Another bad habit.

Again, Hare alone heard this too.

Hyena's turn was not long in the coming either, which Hare also heard.

"Hyena. Ooo ugly, always walking around like he's missing something. Maybe longer hind legs, more spots or maybe a better haircut."

Hippo once more fell over rolling in the dust with laughter.

"Wet, wet, ooo ugly ugly, ugly. anyone ever seen a wet hyena."

Hippo shouting out load for all to hear. Screeching with laughter. Screeching? Yes screeching. It's the strangest sound you ever heard coming from such a large animal as Hippo. But yes, he screeched a high pitch screech.

In this way, Hippo's malicious repartee continued, insulting animal after animal which came to his warped mind. As always, Hare was there to hear.

MIRROR, MIRROR ON THE WATER

ONCE AGAIN, AS BEFORE, Hippo would stare into the waterhole to admire his great beauty, stroking his silky ears while Hare watched in secret.

This time, after stroking his silky ears, he remembered Hare with his ears. The thought of Hare's ears had Hippo rolling about with raucous laughter. No sooner had he done this, when he remembered his own beautiful chestnut fur, smartly straightening up, shaking himself off. Without delay, since it was his way, he went back to staring into the waterhole, to admire his extreme good looks once again.

Again, Hare was there, watching, listening, with ever increasing wonder, curious to what Hippo was laughing at this time.

"Well now Hare! There is a funny looking creature. Hop."

Hippo shouted hop out loud once again. So, he did, hop that is. You should have seen Hippo hop! Then he did it again, then again, no not again, yes again. Hippo laughed so hard he almost fell into the water.

Directly, he stood up, then blow me down, if he did not do it again. Hop that is. Once again Hippo fell over laughing, rolling in the dust.

In the meantime, Hare was taking mental notes of this performance of Hippo with ever increasing anger.

"Can you hear me Hare, with those silly-looking, long, bald ears of yours? Come watch me hop"

You guessed it. He did it again. Hare could keep his peace no longer, shouting at the top of his voice.

"I am right here Hippo."

Hare was standing not three paces away, behind this larger-than-life, egomaniac. Hippo actually jumped with fright! Well now, that was funny.

"Oh, no you, are you into scaring me too. Shame on you Hare."

"Shame on me? After hearing your utterances and nastiness to almost all the animals in the kingdom? I have heard enough. No. Shame on you, you self-opinionated blob"

It had become Hare's turn to be hopping up and down with anger, but at the same time, a bit sorry for what he just said. Although he was determined to see justice done.

"Shame on me you say? We will see about that!"

No sooner said, than he was gone. It was a pretty ruffled Hare, who disappeared into the undergrowth that day.

YES, PLEASE TELL

ON REFLECTION, HARE thought it not unjust to tell the other animals he should happen upon, how he heard Hippo mocking them and in detail as well.

This stirred up a great fuss amid the many animals who were more than familiar with the sort Hippo was turning into. Before a lynch mob could be formed, Lion spoke out with a mighty roar, to address the crowd.

"Before you group take the law into your own hands, listen to my plan. We will have a beauty parade including Hippo, to see who is the handsomest of us all.""

Lion, as you will remember, was wise you know.

"What will be the prize?"

Asked a puzzled Hare, himself thinking, if Hippo should win, we will be worse off than before.

"I know what you are thinking Hare!"

Remember Lion was wise.

"To the one who wins, it will be the duty of all the others to serve that one, from one full moon to the next."

Hare looking at Lion, hoped he had not lost his marbles. But Hare, himself, being kind of wise, decided to leave matters to their leader on a wait and see basis.

The beauty parade took place with much fuss and ado. Needless to say, Hippo won.

LION'S PLAN SPRINGS INTO ACTION

THE PLAN, WHATEVER plan it was Lion hatched, was about to come into play.

"We will make Hippo a great big, comfortable bed, placing much grass beneath the great baobab tree that looks like it was planted upside down. Inclusive, without fail, we will bring Hippo his food and worship him from full moon to full moon. We will wash him, dry him and also brush him down till he shines. Our purpose is to shame Hippo, into not acting so almighty, around us all anymore."

Not all were convinced Lion was right. But as you know, Lion was wise and all the animals agreed to go along with his wise counsel. Wasting no time they set about to do the things Lion advised, as well as doing all of Hippo's bidding, included.

Life went on and needless to say, Hippo got worse in his vanity, insisting those who passed close by, should bow down to him. This caused a great stir among many and it was upon this account Lion was approached with earnest.

"You must do something Lion. I am not given to bowing to anyone, least of all to a wetted mop like Hippo."

This was none other than Elephant with his rightly indignant comment to Lion. Elephant echoed the sentiments of all the other animals.

"Tomorrow I will approach Hippo concerning all our complaints."

That night was full moon and the entire group of animals felt much better about the next day. At some time before midnight, a huge typically African storm arose, lightning striking everywhere. Well, the inevitable was surely soon to happen. Suddenly, lightning struck the great giant tree beneath which Hippo slept.

Hippo woke to fire all around him. His bed was burning. His beautiful hair was burning. The veld around him was burning. The shrubs and trees were burning. Hippo knew the whereabouts of his waterhole, therefore, running for his life, he ran straight through the fire into the water. There he stayed, in a sheer state of shock right through the night, only his eyes, nose and short, hairless ears, showing above the waterline, till morning.

Once the sun rose, the fire was long gone, Hippo emerged early from his waterhole. Looking about to see if anyone was watching. Gingerly, satisfied no one could see him, he climbed out. Once out, he waited for the water to settle before approaching the edge of the pool to see his reflection, as he always did. This time, the shock, the horror, the indignity, insult upon insult, the sight almost scared him out of his wits, he saw not only small bald ears, but turning around he saw his stumpy, hairless tail as well.

"My ears my silky ears, gone, my tail my long glossy tail, also gone, aaah. Whow is me, I am bald and hairless from head to tail, what am I going to do. All the other animals are going to laugh at me."

As for the rest of his pink, hairless body, Hippo was so shocked he dived into the water, never to show himself again, except for his nose, eyes and ears showing above the water.

Now you know why there are no more hairy Hippo's to be found, still to this day.

From that day to this, all hippos only go out to graze at night, although, only well-tanned hippos show themselves on the banks of rivers or waterholes in broad daylight. These mannerisms you will see with all Hippo's descendants to this day.

The moral of the story, you say? Vanity is an enemy of the good, trapping all who fall into its grasp.

CHAPTER 20

MONKEY'S FIDDLE AND BOW

L ong, long, ago somewhere in Africa, when all the people and animals were new. A wonder of nature, a strange phenomenon I venture neither you nor I could have wisely guest to be at all possible.

It may never have crossed your mind to know that the fiddle finds its roots in Africa. Does this matter, probably not to most, but it did to make this tale a reality. Curious as the journey may seem, you are about to embark upon a fable that, would you believe, was said to be mostly true. You be the judge.

Monkey, although a good hunter and careful keeper of his domain, had run out of food to eat, as a result of a harsh drought in his country. The need for food, lead Monkey to seek out his cousin in another part of the world, not overly far from where he lived, but far enough. Hungry and forlorn, the long journey completely exhausted Monkey, happy to have finally arrived at Baboons shelter.

After the long, arduous journey, out of breath and extremely hungry, Monkey looked a mess when he greeted his cousin, falling into his arm.

"Baboon, I never thought I would ever see you again."

"You look like you were dragged through a buffalo thorn tree backwards, my poor cousin. Come, eat something, then it is off to sleep with you, my friend."

Next morning Baboon wanted to know if this was a courtesy visit or maybe something more serious.

"Oh, Baboon my cousin, I wish I had come months ago. My region has been hit by a terrible drought, no matter how little I ate or how carefully I spared my food, things kept getting worse. So here I am as if a beggar at your door too lazy to work."

"You lazy? Never, I know you too well, my cousin. As for now, you are here to stay, as long as the drought in your land continues. You use my domain as if it were your own. As soon as you feel stronger, you can help me gather food."

MONKEY'S NEW BEGINNING

BECAUSE MONKEY WAS family, not merely a guest, he insisted on going to work right away, because family stick together.

"If I collapse, I know you will pick me up Baboon. Where do we begin?"

Baboon taking Monkey, immediately set to work to gather food for them both, no matter who gathered more, they still shared fairly between them.

After many months of the two living like this, news came to Monkey that the drought was broken, food was once more getting plentiful in his own region.

"Well, it seems you will be leaving someday soon, Monkey?"

Baboon really enjoyed having Monkey around. He gave a calming effect to his life, but looking down at himself, he was sure he had gained weight. This day, although a sad one, was filled with excitement. His cousin's leaving was anticipated and he had been waiting for this moment to pass on two special gifts to him.

"Monkey, you know I have travelled most of the known regions of this continent from end to end. Well, while on my travels, I came into contact with two wonders of this world given me by the old man who saved me. The way in which this came to pass, was that I had been captured by hunters, then put into a cage in a market place for sale. The old man passing by took pity on me and bought me. This is the one who took me on all his travels, treating me like one of his own. When time came for him to die, for he was then of a great age, he wanted me to have two highly favoured, special gifts as a legacy."

"What are these gifts Baboon?"

"I am also coming to the end of my days, not too long from now, therefore, I am giving them to you. Without seeing them demonstrated, you cannot know their value. Tomorrow I will show you."

FIDDLE AND BOW LESSONS

THE FOLLOWING DAY EARLY as agreed, the two went out to a secret cave in a tree near Baboons home. Here Baboon fetched two bags well wrapped in waterproof leather skins, which Baboon carefully unwrapped.

"This bow and its arrows, as well as this fiddle with its bow, are sacred, no one knows their origin, although they are ancient, they are still amazingly strong. I have twice in my lifetime needed the bow and arrows to feed myself. Although the fiddle, I have never been unfortunate enough to need. I will teach you how they work because they are extremely special."

Baboon first brought out the bow and its arrows. Seeing a sizeable fig high in a nearby tree, he pointed the arrow in its general direction without really aiming, shooting down the fig with one shot. Monkey ran to fetch it, picking it up he noticed the arrow straight through the middle, he was amazed at such a wonder. Then Baboon let Monkey shoot down the next fig himself after showing him how to hold the bow, as well as load the arrow correctly. This done, Monkey took his first shot, low-and-behold down came the fig, arrow and all, shot right through the middle. Monkey was overjoyed at such a wonder as this. Jumping up and down with excitement. Baboon remembering what the old man warned him, he, in turn, warned his cousin not to ever use this gift unwisely. In the day that he did, the power in the bow would become lost to him forever.

"As I told you earlier in tears. So, I tell you again. Please do not forget, only ever use this bow with its arrows for an emergency when you are in great need. Like the need, you had when you came here so hungry, or the power will be lost to you, never to work for you again."

When Monkey was well versed in the use of his one gift. Baboon was ready to show Monkey his other life-saving gift, pulling the fiddle and bow out of the other bag.

"Monkey this fiddle is even more wonderful than the bow and its arrows. This fiddle my happy cousin will make anything dance when the player is in great need. Never doubting its powerful properties, this instrument must be played accompanied with much meaning and love, for it to work."

Baboon in a sombre mind proceeded to demonstrate to Monkey how the fiddle was held, then he played. No sooner did Baboon begin to play, when his arm and fingers were led by the tune. Monkey, joined by the birds in the trees, began to dance as if in a trance, while Baboon happily played away in remembrance of his long-lost friend who had given him this special gift. Becoming carried away by the powerful moment, he forgot this was a demonstration to teach Monkey. Stopping short when he remembered, the many dancers around him came to an abrupt halt. Instantly the happy dancers cried out at once.

"Give us more, give us more."

The moment Monkey started to play as his cousin had shown him, Baboon, joined the birds in the trees who once again began to dance all around Monkey as he played. Monkey became quite carried away with his new present, when suddenly recalling Baboon's age he quickly stopped.

"My dear cousin Baboon, you have blessed me with two of the most wonderful gifts anyone could ever have. Thank you, thank you."

Monkey was naturally over the moon with excitement and gratitude. While the two were walking back to Baboons place, Baboon once again warned Monkey only to use any one of his new possessions when he was in dire straits. He also warned his cousin to keep them in good condition by cleaning them regularly. Making sure they were kept in a safe and secure place, away from any prying eyes or hands. This was all for his own good.

It had become time for Monkey to return home. Early the next morning Monkey bid Baboon goodbye, knowing he may not see his cousin ever again. Monkey bearing mixed emotions of sorrow and joy went on his way back home. Carrying with him his two precious gifts in a sack over his shoulder, well-hidden, disguised by his kind cousin.

Monkey, on the road again, but this time with a spring in his step. Well taken care of, thanks to Baboon's hospitality.

MONKEY'S FATEFUL RETURN HOME

ON HIS RETURN AND ALMOST home the first one he met was Gorilla. He was not too fond of Gorilla, marking him with caution. Happily, the old sage of a Gorilla brought Monkey up to date concerning the latest news in the district.

Although he mumbled a complaint about certain tasty fruits growing high in the trees, he could not reach without the branches breaking. Monkey reasoned this being an older Gorilla, more stable in his ways, was most likely to be straight forward. Monkey, I imagine had too much time to think while listening to Gorilla, somewhat forgetting his cousin's stern warnings.

Carelessly boasting, Monkey, proud of his new acquisitions, thought it no problem to show off to Gorilla what the weapon he had in his sack could do. Pulling out the bow with its arrows from their bag. He also haughtily boasted what they would do in the hands of someone possessing deft and style. Swaggering as he went with bow in hand, he asked Gorilla to point out the fruits to him.

No sooner did Gorilla point out the biggest of the fruits high up in the tree, when it went down. Shocked, Gorilla wanted to know how he did that. Monkey never answered. Gorilla in disbelief, ran to where the fruit had fallen, sure enough, there it was, an arrow straight through the middle.

It was not long before Gorilla made a great meal out of many other fruits his simian friend shot down for him. Monkey was not taken by the way Gorilla was eyeing his bow and arrows with bad intent. Also, how he never bothered to thank him for the meal he just gave him. The little primate, suddenly conscious of his error, started putting his special gift back in its sack.

Gorilla, wasted no time begging Monkey to give him the weapon. When Monkey refused, Gorilla became aggressive toward his host. Knowing Gorilla's strength, being considerably superior to his own, made him more, than a little worried for his safety

CHIMPANZEE TO THE RESCUE OR NOT

WHILE STOIC MONKEY tussled with Gorilla over his gift, Chimpanzee happened by.

Monkey, greatly relieved, was hoping Chimpanzee, although a distant cousin, would be an ally. Yet out of the blue, before either had even greeted their new guest. Gorilla blurted out to Chimpanzee, how Monkey had stolen his bow and arrows.

Monkey was shattered, Gorilla would tell such a story. Immediately, Chimpanzee told Monkey to give Gorilla back his sack at once. Monkey refused, telling Chimpanzee his side of the story. Chimpanzee, after hearing Monkey, informed them both he was unqualified to make a decision. This matter actually called for the big gathering, in the debate at the big boma.

Chimpanzee, however, declared he would have to secure the objects in question till the day of the gathering. With the sack in his possession, Chimpanzee immediately ran off hunting fruit near and far, leaving a path of destruction in his wake everywhere he went, in search of more fun.

Monkey, upset about the needless waste, was worried his weapon would lose its powers. Therefore he went to Lion, head of the council of animals, telling him the story concerning Gorilla and Chimpanzee. Lion did not believe Monkey's story but told him to appear at the big animal gathering to give his story and there to let the council decide the outcome. In the meantime, he confiscated the evidence from Chimpanzee for the day of the hearing at the gathering.

THE ANIMAL COUNCIL

FINALLY, THE DAY FOR Monkey to appear before the great gathering in the big boma arrived. Monkey was asked to tell his story first. After him came Chimpanzee, with a testimony aimed to weaken Monkey's case. Because he not only went against his distant cousin but sided with Gorilla, hoping by doing so, he could get the bow and arrows for himself.

Then it came to Gorilla to give his version of things, which was nothing but one lie after another. Poor Monkey's evidence was not looking too good at all. Then Lion spoke up.

"Monkey, do you have anything else you want to say in your defence before the council give their verdict?"

Monkey pleaded, he had a witness in Baboon, who they could ask, it was he who gave him that bow and arrows as a gift of friendship.

"Where is Baboon."

"He is at his home far away."

Lion conferred with the assembly, who refused on the grounds that 'Monkey was trying to delay his sentence' by lying. The council reminded Monkey, he should have brought Baboon as his witness when he came before them, in the first place.

After the three testimonies were carefully considered, there was much deliberation by the animal assembly, who gave the verdict of death to Monkey, by hanging from the neck, till he was dead.

Theft you see was a terrible offence among the animal kingdom. Therefore death was the only verdict.

Out of desperation for justice, Monkey's thoughts were jarred by what his cousin Baboon had taught him, remembering his fiddle, which still hung by his side.

Monkey made his request to the council to play his fiddle. After some debate, more as a favour from the gathering, Monkey's request was granted, giving him permission to play a tune on his fiddle as his last wish.

The charm, the emotion, the mastery of the fiddle in Monkey's hands, brought out all the powers of this wonderful instrument with one who now played like a maestro. One who's heart was almost broken by the lies that came against him. Monkey's deeply sorrowful heart, with a death sentence over his head, produced a musical wonder, stirring up the entire gathering, who whooshed around him like a whirlwind in a trance. Stomping around, and around, and around they went, kicking up dust throughout the big boma. First, a slow stomp which grew in ever-increasing speed, it was clear Monkey and his fiddle had become one, in a crescendo of mesmerising sounds. Oblivious to the exhausted animals falling all around him, legs still gyrating in the air, Monkey played on and on. Everywhere, from the hills to the valleys, was filled with music. Still, Monkey played, himself transfixed by those sweet sounds coming from his miraculous fiddle. Who could stop him now?

Gorilla was the first to cry out in breathless pleading tones for Monkey to stop. His heart, breaking with remorse, while his old legs were shaking him to pieces as he lay there in a convulsive mess on his back.

Monkey, conscious of nothing but the fiddle went on, hearing only the stomping of his own feet. And so, Monkey played on and on and on, his arm gliding his bow ever faster over the strings of his beloved fiddle. A great peace came over Monkey as he played, an overwhelming peace that no one could take away from him this time.

Then Lion tripping over his wife's feet one time too many, growling out to Monkey in a loud roar as he went past while Mrs Lion hung onto his mane for dear life. Lion offering Monkey his whole kingdom, if he would only stop playing this now menacing fiddle. Monkey shouted back at Lion, who at this stage was almost crawling on the floor, with Mrs Lion still tugging out his mane, shuddering as she danced. Monkey slowed to inform Lion, he wanted his name cleared, his bow and arrows returned and he could keep his kingdom. Still playing on, he said he wanted an apology from Gorilla and Chimpanzee for their lying, as well as repentance for stealing it from him.

Gorilla and Chimpanzee cried out as one voice, screaming for forgiveness. Lion withdrew the sentence, with an ear-splitting roar, which could possibly have been heard across his whole kingdom. Monkey stopped.

The moment he stopped playing, the entire kingdom scattered, sending animals to all parts of the world, in their effort to get away from Monkey and his lethal fiddle. Never daring to look back in case he began again. Since then, every kind of animal has been found in all parts of the world to this day.

The moral of the story, you say? Never underestimate the power of music.

CHAPTER 21

THE MOUTHFUL OF MIRACLES

Long, long, ago somewhere in Africa, when all the people and animals were new. There were places in the world where life did not follow the norm. In Africa, it was better understood that there was no normal. Life in this continent has always made up its own mind, dancing to its own drum, according to the dictates of tradition rather than deliberate governmental order.

Keeping this in mind will help the reader understand the uniqueness of this tradition in Africa. It is with this awareness that this story should be read.

A young wife went to live in a certain village with her husband where every marriage was happy, except hers. It was the place of her husband's employ. Therefore, she made the best of what she had, taking care of him as best she knew how. But as hard as she tried, she could not make him happy.

She was unlike the other woman in her village, who saw her as the odd one out. They ignored her most of the time, even crossing the road when they saw her coming along. To add to her misery, she wanted children, but her husband would not hear of it. He insisted their relationship would need to make some big changes before he would entertain such a thought as children. Yet, the harder she tried, the worse their relationship became, even though she believed she was the perfect wife.

THE HAPPY OLD LADY

MONTHS PASSED AND EVEN having done all she could, things became worse instead of better. In desperation one day, she related her story in confidence to the local herbal doctor, to whom she had gone for help. When she finished her tale, he suggested her best course of action, would be to consult the oldest woman in their village, who also had the longest marriage of all the residents.

Without losing a moment, off, she went to knock on the old lady's door. The door opened to reveal a graceful, kind-looking old woman with a handsome upright stature smiling at her.

"Good morning, my child. How can I help you?"

"Forgive my tears. I have been advised to speak to you regarding my failing marriage."

"Please come in, take a seat."

Within moments, the young wife had launched into the tale of her unhappy, crumbling marriage to the most unreasonable and irritating man who could ever have been created. Tears ran unabated down her cheeks as she related the stories of her awful life, enduring this monster of an individual, she was forced to live with. She told how they shouted and screamed, throwing things around the house only to have her husband walk off, leaving her in despair.

All the while, the old woman did not say a word but sat patiently and quietly listening to her story. She told how he always did the opposite of what she expected, deliberately, to make her angry. He was inconsiderate, with a controlling, ungrateful nature, even staying away from home, coming in late at night without eating his supper. He would get into bed without a greeting. Ignoring her, he would go to sleep, not even saying 'thank you' for the uneaten dinner she laboured so hard to make for him. This would happen so often, she decided to only make dinner when he came home at a reasonable time.

She told the old woman she was afraid her husband might be having an affair. This last bit made her sob even louder. While she soaked up her kerchief with tears, the old lady patted her on the shoulder, with the most consoling words.

"Never mind, we will fix this, my child. I have a remedy which has worked for all the women of this village with bad husbands."

"Oh, can you really help? I am desperate."

"I can see that, my dear."

It was then the old lady told the young wife how she must use the miracle water that she would give her. This precious liquid came from a secret fountain, deep within the forest adjoining their village.

"This water is what brought happiness to the other marriages in the village, my child. It is this you need to solve your problems once and for all. But there is one important thing for success you must do for yourself."

"What is that? I am prepared for great suffering if it means it will save my marriage and I can have children."

Giving the young wife a water bag full of water to hold, the old lady proceeded to give her the instructions on how to use it.

"You must look out for your husband at the times he comes home. Here is what is important for you to do. Make and eat your food before your husband gets home. Before he comes in the door, you take a mouthful of this water, and then keep it in your mouth as long as you can. If you need to swallow, refill your mouth and remember to do this till he goes to sleep. Only then can you have your mouth without water in it.

In the morning, before he rises, make his breakfast. When he comes to eat, take a mouthful of the water and only swallow it when he is out of sight. If at any time there is a need for you to swallow the water, immediately take another mouthful. While your husband is nearby, always keep your mouth full of miracle water.

There is enough water in this water bag for a two-week supply if you obey my instructions. At the end of two weeks, come back to me for a new supply of water, while you bring me up to date with news of your husband's progress."

Before the young wife left, the kind old lady smiled, reminding her once more to follow her instructions to the letter, if she wanted to teach her husband the lesson he needs. The young wife thanked the old woman, wondering how hard it could be to accomplish such an easy task as she had? She left the happy old lady, eagerly longing for the evening to come. She would teach that wretched husband of hers a lesson he was not going to forget in a hurry.

SIMPLE DOES NOT MEAN EASY

THE YOUNG WIFE MUSED with inner confidence, as she made her way back home. Her husband was about to get what was coming to him, just as the other husbands of her village had been fixed.

When she arrived home, she went to work immediately, making dinner. When completed, having eaten herself, she waited by the window looking out for her husband, to be sure she was ready. When she saw him come up the pathway, she took a mouthful of the precious water.

In he came, storming straight past her without so much as a greeting. Hanging up his hat and sitting down at his plate, he began to eat. She wanted to ask him where his manners were, but for the sake of the water, she remained silent.

The whole evening, she did all the necessary things she thought her husband would want. Her aim was to stop him from starting any argument, thereby endangering her precious mouthful of water. Noticing her unusual silence, he asked after her health and if she was ill. Smiling and shaking her head, she went off to wash the dishes.

As usual, her husband was his old annoying self, not thanking her for dinner or noticing the things she did for him, or offering to help with the dishes. While she dried the dishes, she came to the conclusion this task the old woman gave her, was harder than she first anticipated. Nevertheless, the night ended up being a success as did the next and so on.

As the days went by, the young wife got better at judging the needs of her husband before he asked or made a rude remark. She became determined to prove to the old lady that her husband was more than a lost cause and nothing like the other men in the village. So, with this resolve, she pressed on till the end of the two weeks, knowing she would win and prove her point.

When she arrived at the old lady for her refill of water, she launched into what the two weeks had produced. She rattled away on how she was winning and her husband was even showing signs of cracking under her silence from the first day.

What she disliked most was how he was now turning to sarcasm, even thanking her for things she did for him, which he never did before. But she was determined to push on, even in the face of his odd false favours around the house. This he had never done before. As if he cared what the house looked like!

Nevertheless, things were playing into her hands, getting some improvements done for a change. She remarked to the old woman how she could not thank him for fear of losing her mouthful of water, which suited her. Because she was not stupid, she was sure he was only doing those things to get compliments from her anyway.

"I believe I am winning and teaching that husband of mine a valuable lesson."

"My dear child, things appear to be going as planned, so keep up the good work. Here, take for yourself another bag of water."

After more encouragement from the happy old lady, the young wife returned home, confident she was surely winning.

DINNER WITH A DIFFERENCE

WHILE PREPARING DINNER that evening, she was surprised by her husband coming in the kitchen door early, holding out a bunch of her favourite flowers he must have picked from the forest. With no water in her mouth, she pretended to have a mouthful.

"You have turned into the most beautiful, kind wife a man could ask for. I have brought you these flowers to say thank you and sorry for not allowing us to have children. I have changed my mind. Will you accept these flowers as a token of my love for you and to tell you I would like us to have children if this is still your wish?"

The young wife burst into tears, hugging her husband with all her might.

"Oh, yes, yes, my gentle, handsome husband, it is still my wish. I am sorry for the way I have treated you all this time and I have long dreamed of what beautiful children we would make."

"It is settled then. I know what you have been doing concerning the mouthful of water and how hard the last two weeks must have been for you."

"When did you find out and how?"

"Today, when I saw you leaving the old lady's house with the bag of water. I asked one of my friends who told me the story about the mouthful of miracle water. I straightway went to the forest and picked you these flowers, which I now think need some water themselves."

Smiling, the young wife gratefully took the bunch of flowers from her husband's hand. Ironically, she arranged them in a vase filled with miracle water, placing them on the dining table where most of their past battles had taken place.

This happy circumstance changed both their lives forever. They had the most beautiful children who all grew up into a large family with many descendants, of whom I am one. And the young wife herself became the old lady who helped thousands of marriages to happiness, for as long as she lived.

The moral of the story, you say? Never despair when the ugly duckling takes a long time to turn into a swan. One day, your love will bear the fruit befitting your patience.

CHAPTER 22

WHY WARTHOG WALKS ON HIS KNEES

Long, long, ago somewhere in Africa, when all the people and animals were new. Far into the green desert, our warthog found an old abandoned anthill, which once was home to an enormous colony of termites, but Aardwolf had eaten most of the termites with their queen. So, when the remaining termites lost their queen, they left the empty mound behind.

This old anthill, Warthog turned into a roomy, comfortable lair. By digging out around the opening which Aardwolf originally made, he made a spacious entryway. Warthog was awfully proud of his impressive home, standing at the entrance, nose in the air, as the other animals passed by, on their way to the water hole. He was more than satisfied, no other animal possessed such a magnificent home as he did.

One day, Warthog, as usual, was standing in the vestibule of his burrow, as he was want to do when to his horror, he saw a huge lion coming straight toward his grand foyer. Warthog began backing away, but then he suddenly realised, his splendid entrance was now so big, Lion would have no problem fitting in, trapping him inside.

"Aiy, yaiy, yaiy. Lion will eat me in my own lounge! This calls for emergency action?"

Warthog moaned under his breath in terror. Then a story came to mind. He remembered an old trick against a lion he had heard Jackal boasting about. Could it work again? Thinking to himself, with little time to play and rushed with no better plan in mind, being under enormous pressure, in horrible circumstances, he had no choice with nothing to lose, or so he thought.

WARTHOG TRIES TO IMITATE JACKAL

WARTHOG STRUGGLED AND strained as he pretended to be holding up the roof of his den with his strong back. Pushing up hard knowing Lion was watching and on his way, leaving him no time. But in his fright, when he hatched his fateful plan to trick Lion, he got the story back-to-front from the way Jackal told it.

"Help! I am going to be crushed! The roof is collapsing! Flee, oh, mighty Lion, before you are crushed along with me!"

Now Lion is no fool, yet some even say Lion, as you know, is wise. This time it was a giveaway. He stopped to stare at Warthog, shaking his head at the reasoning of the poor creature. Warthog was totally unaware that Lion was not in the slightest bit of danger if his roof did cave in. Lion also realised Warthog was using Jackal's old trick but confused himself in his fright. Facing him, he roared so ferociously Warthog dropped to his knees, quaking from fear, begging for mercy.

Dim-witted Warthog had good fortune that day. Lion was in one of his better moods and not in the least bit hungry, having just eaten. So, he forgave the warthog with a parting instruction to keep for the rest of his life.

"Stay on your knees, you foolish creature and in future, whenever you see me go by, this is the way I want to see you behave."

As he carried on his journey to the water, Lion laughed to himself, shaking his shaggy head as he went.

Warthog took Lion's command to heart. This is why, to this day, you will see Warthog's descendants in truly humiliating postures, with bottoms up in the air, snout's snuffling in the dust, feeding on their knees.

The moral of the story, you say? If you behave like a fool, you will be treated like a fool.

CHAPTER 23

JABU AND THE LION

Long, long, ago somewhere in Africa, when all the people and animals were new. The truly brave heroes of the African tribes were the herdsman, who without much reward, faced great dangers to save their animals.

Why keep cattle in a land abundant in wildlife? Rather, let me not get ahead of myself here. Consider the needs of the people in their day, as this is primarily what our tale is about. From the herds of domesticated animals would come milk, meat, ropes, fat, oil, mats, clothing, shields and in fact, much more than this simple story involves. Here we are not talking of wool, yarn or lanolin, these belong to another story.

You say hunters would provide most of this too? Of course! Although, the domestic herds provided an essential contribution western cultures overlook, which is lobola. An important something the hunters could not give the people and that something, they themselves needed. Lobola! An essential something without which a man and woman were forbidden to get married or start a family, so here is where the humble herder plays such an important role.

Lobola was a traditional African custom, involving the trading of a suitor's wealth in cattle for a chosen wife of his desire. A suitor was required by tribal law to pay the father of the bride-to-be a certain number of cattle for his daughter's hand in marriage. Her final value in cattle would then be argued out, to be decided upon between the parties involved. In the form of simple economics, herds and wealth were added to the tribe.

In this way, the wild animals were preserved in favour of the cattle grazing side by side with them.

Hence, as you can see, this reveals a better collective idea of the value of the herders of old and of this story too. Key to the success of any tribe chiefly belonged to these young men and upon this matter, I will not expound. Nay, by way of this African fable, I will let the story tell the story.

This folktale sings the praises of these brave young men out in the wilds of Africa and in so doing, tells a younger generation of how things in times past were upheld and administered.

To single out an example of the herdsman's courage, dedication and service, has not been easy. There are many heroes among the simple animal keepers of old, but one story stands out above the rest. This is the tale of a young man named Jabu and his strange encounter with a lion.

Jabu, a herdsman of a certain village, somewhere in Africa, shone out as a special young man. Presently fourteen, having started at the age of eight, he learned his trade in the traditional manner from the older herdsman. So here, chosen above the rest, is Jabu's story.

JABU THE HERDER

JABU PROVED HIMSELF unmatched in cattle herding for his region. This young man possessed a special love for animals, tame or wild, although he much preferred cattle to other domesticated types, like donkeys or goats. His special love for cattle was naturally developed, in that his father had the largest number of these animals in their village.

Jabu also had the most sisters, for whom his father received a lot of lobola over the years of his upbringing. This gave Jabu's farther a well-stocked cattle herd, for which the young man was made responsible.

Jabu knew one day his turn to pay lobola would come, but for the time being, looking after the cattle was the more important. What mattered, apart from good grazing, was keeping the herds safe from the many predators, like the crocodiles lurking on the river banks, when the animals were taken down to drink. To top this, was the all-day vigil for a lion, a leopard, or hyena attack on the young. This watchfulness never let up, including while herding them to and from safe pastures.

On a day much like any other warm, sunny African day, one could find Jabu sitting well elevated in a tall shady tree minding the herds, his trusted sling and assegai always close at hand. This day, he quietly carved away on an exotic scented piece of wood, intended as a gift for one of his sisters, whose coming marriage would bring more lobola for him to look after.

From his vantage point, his sharp eyes flicked to a movement far in the distance. Coming toward him, he saw someone running swiftly through the bush, from the direction of his village. When the runner got closer, he recognised the figure from his running style to be that of his life-long friend, Sipho, a fellow herdsman.

He became concerned. Sipho was shouting something while he ran, which Jabu could not make out. When his friend came near, he recognised the word "lion" repeated over and over. Sipho, out of breath, seeing the puzzled look on his friend's face as he came closer, tied to explain better, his chest heaving as he gasped for air. Then he started.

"There is... a lion Jabu... a big lion... down by the river!"

"When? What lion?"

"The hunters say... it is the one... who killed... Thabo's fathers' calf. You must save your cows right away!"

"The lion will not attack now, it has eaten its fill for the day."

Jabu wisely answered his friend, while he quietly pondered the lion's movements from the spoor he had been checking, over the past two days.

Jabu knew lions mainly hunted at night unless wounded or troubled by some malady. He found a lion like this last year, which he stunned with his sling before some of the older herdsmen stabbed it to death with long spears. The lion skin was then cured and given to the chief by the herders.

"Sipho, do you remember the lion from last year?"

Sipho remembered, then launched into an explanation of how the men of the village were right then making a large snare for this lion.

"We will give the chief this skin as well when he is caught. Bring your cattle to the boma, come see."

"I do not think it is fair for the lion to die. It was Thabo's fault for leaving the calf out of the boma that night. Therefore, as a result of his carelessness, the lion must die. My cattle will graze and have water as usual, before I put them into the boma early for the night like you have done. You know me, Sipho."

"I know you, my friend, which is the reason I came to warn you. See you later at the fire. I am going back to see the snare they are making."

THE LION TRAP

SCATTERED ACROSS A fading savannah sky, the sun's rays plied red streaks onto snow-white clouds. The thudding and shuffling sound of restless cattle below his tree drew Jabu back from a far-away dreamland. The day well spent, the young man looked up at fast-approaching dusk, contentedly he smiled to himself, climbing down from his tree. Whistling for the other scattered animals to come home, the herd followed closely as he led them on to the river for their evening drink. As always, he watchfully surveyed the bush, then more carefully when they came closer to the river.

When he arrived, he met the other herders already watering their animals. While his cattle drank, he kept a keen eye out for crocodile on the far bank of the river. Jabu was a clever, skilled, herder, bringing his cattle in last, knowing the crocodile usually attack the first animals to come to the water. He preferred his herd to eat their fill before leading them to drink. When the cattle finished drinking, Jabu led them home to their boma for the night.

The main talk around the fire that night was of the lion and the big pen which had been built on the river bank. Jabu had not seen this new contraption, although he planned to be there first thing in the morning to check if the lion was caught. From the hunter's descriptions, he had a fair idea where the snare was set, but not its exact location. Large amounts of meat were cut from the partly eaten calf, to be used as bait in the snare for luring the lion inside. Therefore, he was confident the lion should be caught sometime in the night.

On such occasions, an old custom was employed. Using a donkey, the entrails of the carcass were dragged along the ground from where the original kill was made, up to the entrance of the snare. This method proved the most successful with preceding generations of hunters, given that the killer would simply think its kill walked away, dying somewhere else and follow the scent. Human scent was reduced to a minimum, by the donkey being ridden while it pulled the entrails. The meat inside the trap was set up in such a way, the instant the lion took hold of it, the trapdoor would shut down fast, locking it inside.

When Jabu finished eating his evening meal, he went to lie on his mat by the fire to listen to the old men as they spoke of this, that and many other tales, to do with this wonderful world in which he lived. While he lay there listening to the hum of voices, he stared up into the night-time sky, curiously thinking of where the lion might be right then, still deep in thought, looking far into the stars, he fell asleep.

Early in the morning, before anyone except the night watch was awake, Jabu rounded up his cattle from the boma, leading them to the river to drink. After having their fill, Jabu again gathered them together. This time, taking them on to the grasslands to graze.

On his way down to the river, even though he vigilantly searched, Jabu did not find the lion pen at the places he most reckoned it to be. On their way to the grazing veld, our young herder became far more watchful in his search as they next passed close by some dense undergrowth.

Out of nowhere, the still morning air was shattered by a hair-raising vibration. The sound of a mighty roar froze the cattle wild-eyed, legs spread in their tracks. The ground shook, gripping Jabu's heart, paralysing him where he stood. It took more than a moment for him to regain his composure. Ducking down on his haunches, clutching his assegai in his right hand, he hurriedly groped for the sling hanging around his neck with his left hand.

Meanwhile, the cattle shuffled backwards leaving their leader alone. Rooted to the spot, down on one knee, his eyes scanned the dark early morning shadows under the thicket, seeing nothing. This lion was close, Jabu could smell it. In the cool dank still air, he could hear his heart beating as it banged against his ribs.

"This lion is near, but is it caught?"

Little sun, no sign, nothing! The fingers of his right hand squeezed the shaft of his assegai even tighter. His sling lying on the ground at his feet, he slowly used his left hand to search for a river rock in the pouch hanging by his side, the whole while his eyes darted to and fro, piercing the darkness. Adjusting his thoughts, he abandoned the sling idea, seeing the thick bush was too close, looping it slowly back around his neck. Mumbling quietly to himself, he became concerned for the cattle, somewhere behind him.

"Where is this lion? Is it stalking the calves?"

When it came, it bowled him over, like the blast from a strong wind! Jabu was rocked off his haunches from another earth-shaking roar. His legs instinctively launching him backwards, only to land on his back. Flipping quickly onto his belly, he lay there motionless. Finding himself more on the lion's level, his eyes were adjusting better to the darkness, then he saw it. Framed by a hefty black mane, with empty yellow eyes, which seemed to consume the very darkness itself, staring at him, gripping the young man's soul. Transfixed he stared as puffs of steam issued from the lions open mouth in rhythmic pants, scarlet tinged foam mixed in drool, dripping down from wounded gums. His once white teeth stained dark pink by cuts from the bars of a well-constructed prison. Crouched down low, Jabu realised this lion had been eyeing him and the cattle the entire time. Well camouflaged, in its interwoven greenery, Jabu carefully made it out, this was indeed the pen, with the lion held prisoner inside.

Much relieved, Jabu came to his feet, still hunched forward clutching his assegai. He moved cautiously, looking for any other lions on the loose, who may have been attracted by the smell of meat. Constantly he kept watch on the lion in the trap with anxious suspicion as he moved. Taking great care, he slowly moved closer, still wondering to himself. 'Is this lion really caught?'

JABU FACES UP TO LION

AS THE YOUNG MAN APPROACHED, he heard the lion muttering to himself something involving humans catching him in that thing he was in, hoping the boy had come to set him free from a bondage meant for another.

"It is called a trap! The thing you are in. It is a trap for lions like you, who kill innocent tame animals."

This time, it was the lion's turn to jump back. After gaining his composure, he quizzed the boy.

"Oh, how strange, so you can understand me then? My name is Lion, what is yours?"

"None of your business."

Snapped Jabu, still angry at the lion for scaring him so badly.

"Listen, boy. Can you get me out of this thing?"

"I said it is called a trap, not a thing and for good reason too. Well, for your information, I am not a boy, I am a man in our culture."

"Alright, alright, a trap then. And a nasty one at that, too. But I did ask you kindly to let me out."

"Kindly, you call that kindly? You never even said please."

"Ahumm... ahumm... All right... please... will you let me out? Now can we go then?"

"Not so fast. Go where?"

"You said if I said please! And I did."

Lion snapped back, more growling than asking.

"See what I mean. You have a nasty temper, not to be trusted."

"Did you not hear me? I did say please you know."

"I heard you and I am still thinking. Are you to be trusted?"

"Ahh, not easily... but when I give a promise, I never break that. After all, I am a king, you know. Also, for your information, I am the king of all the beasts, well around here anyway."

This last part changed Jabu's thinking. The whole time, he actually wanted to let the lion out, on account of his hatred for any kind of cruelty and this was, after all, the king of the beasts.

"It would have to be a binding promise if I am to let you out, Lion. I value my own life, as does my father and mother, not to mention friends as well as the animals I look after. And you cannot eat any of my cattle either. And you will have to promise to leave the district, never to come back again. Otherwise, I will be letting you out for nothing but trouble."

"Leave the district? But I was born here, like you, I also had a family and so on."

"It is that or nothing. The hunters will soon be here."

Jabu was getting impatient, the hunters should be coming after hearing the roars.

"The hunters! Oops, I nearly forgot about the hunters. Please, boy, let me out. I promise to do everything you asked. As king of the beasts. I promise not to eat you or your animals. I promise to leave the district too. Quick, hurry boy, I hear the hunters coming."

Then Jabu moved swiftly, pulling the trapdoor up for Lion to get out. Jabu, Lion and the cattle quickly moved on toward the grazing veld. When they reached the grazing, Jabu bade Lion goodbye, reminding him of his promise, bidding him on his way, with a sweep of his hand. He was making the cattle nervous. Besides, Jabu noticed the strange manner in which he was looking at him, therefore he was keen to have him gone. At this juncture Lion squared up, looking straight at Jabu, his evil intent clearly visible in those empty yellow eyes. Lion moved ever closer, Jabu, wisely moving backwards, assegai on the ready.

"Remember, for your freedom, you made a king's promise, Lion. I have an assegai, remember?"

"That thing cannot frighten me, especially in the hands of a boy."

"My name is Jabu, I am not boy."

"Huh... now you tell me when it no longer matters."

"Are you the king of the beasts or not? Did you not make a promise as king, to spare my life, those of the animals and leave the district? Promises must never be broken, especially not by kings. You will suffer many things if you break a promise. The hunters will know you attacked me and they will hunt you down."

"You talk too much, young man."

Lion crouched down on his belly, digging his claws deep into the earth, set to attack. Jabu, firmly grasping his assegai, on the ready.

JABU LEARNS A LESSON

AS IF APPEARING OUT of nowhere, Jackal moseyed by, breaking the tense silence.

"Hope I am not troubling anyone, but I heard there was a dead cow somewhere hereabouts to nibble on."

Jackal, studiously perused the undergrowth, in his pretence of ignoring them both, he sniffed around, scratching the ground here and there. Kicking up some dust for extra effect, he was behaving like a regular pest trying to draw attention to himself.

"No, the meat from the cow was used to catch Lion here and the hunters have taken away the rest."

This was all Jabu could think of saying, unexpectedly relieved, at the same time, overwhelmed by the prospect of an ally in Jackal, with Lion turning so treacherously against him.

As you can imagine, Lion's demeanour towards Jackal was somewhat different. Facing Jackal with a sneering growl, which curled up his lips, displaying his gums and showing off his fangs. A gesture which was intended for Jackal to keep on going his way.

"My, sorry to disturb. I was just leaving Lion, so keep your claws to yourself."

"Wait, Jackal, do not go! I am Jabu, the one being wronged here. Lion wants to eat me, even after I freed him from a big trap which has a lot of cow's meat in it. For this, he promised not to harm me or my cattle and leave the district."

Jabu blurted this out somewhat loader than intended, hoping Jackal would take the bait regarding the spare cow's meat. Lion may have picked up on the hint, shuffling forward.

"Run along Jackal, this is none of your business."

Ignoring Lion, Jackal turned to the young man.

"Ooh, I liked that last bit. Leave the district, you say? Lots of meat? Well, I suppose it depends upon how the promise was made then, does it not? Why, which one of you made the promise? Breaking a promise... that is a serious matter,"

As if he never knew who made the promise. It was not hard for Jackal to ponder the virtues of getting involved.

"Yes, yes, yes, so he said. Now get on with it. Listen to his story, while I wait my turn."

Lion straightened up once more, this time menacingly observing Jackal.

"As Lion said, tell me the promise. I am looking out for you as well as for the young man, Lion."

"I still think you to be a meddling little sneak, not to be trusted."

Lion remember, was supposed to be wise, and not easily fooled. Then, with a deep sigh, he lay down, rolling his eyes upwards while he slowly folded his paws one upon another, he then rested his head on them to listen. All the while, he flexed his claws slowly in and out.

"Go ahead Jabu, Lion is waiting."

"Lion made the promise, wanting me to set him free."

After his introduction, Jabu launched into his story for Jackal, telling the whole matter, as it happened between him and Lion at the snare. He further explained what brought about the promise made by Lion in the first place.

"But Lion wants to eat me, breaking his promise. So, Jackal, is that fair? Does Lion have the right to eat the one who saved him?"

Jabu had certainly gotten Jackal's attention.

"I cannot believe it. What a crazy story. Well now Lion, can this young man be telling me, you, king, the wisest, toughest animal of us all, caught in a manmade pen? Surely not?"

"I was! Like I said to start with, it was none of your business. Now scat!"

"Lion, you are going to be the laughing stock of all the animals when I tell them this one."

Jackal sniggered at Lion, falling about, rolling in the sand with laughter.

Lion was greatly angered by Jackal's antics. Springing to his feet, he let out a snappy roar, scaring away a whole group of cattle who were standing nearby chewing the cud, while straining to hear.

"Very well little Jackal, come along, I will show you. This is no ordinary trap but in fact, a huge cunning device not ever seen before. Well, not by me at any rate. When you have seen it, you can run along, leaving me in peace with my meal once more."

"I accept."

Meanwhile, as you know, the cattle had been milling around waiting for a favourable verdict from Jackal, so they could go back to grazing in peace. With Lion, keeping Jabu in front of him, he led Jackal to the snare. While the cattle followed dejectedly at a short distance.

LION'S LAST LESSON

ON THEIR ARRIVAL AT the snare, Jackal was first to speak.

"Lion, you cannot tell me, this strange-looking contraption could actually hold you? Never! I just cannot imagine it. Lion, would it trouble you to pose inside? Only for a moment, then I can get the idea of how the promise came about, plus under what circumstances it was made. From this, I can get a better idea of who might be right in our little puzzle. Thereby I can make a proper judgment."

"I cannot believe you are asking me to do such a stupid, crazy, thing. That is a trap. It is called a trap because it snares animals like me, this after a long nights suffering, I cannot forget. Now you Jackal, are irritating me, as well as preventing me from enjoying a nice quiet snack, eating this young man right here. You have seen the pen, so be gone with you."

Lion, the entire time was taking great care to stay a respectable distance away from that ugly, dangerous thing.

"Ahh, I am sorry my king, I will soon be on my way. I must apologise for being unable to help you anymore Jabu, Lion will not assist us further."

The taunt of Jackal was clearly apparent to Jabu when he looked once more into the snare, before turning to address Lion.

"First, before I leave, pardon me Lion for troubling you, but I see you have left a few choice pieces of meat in this 'so-called trap' of yours. May I help myself, since they will only go begging for nothing?"

Lion slowly turned to look towards the snare, ever mindful to keep a safe distance from that dreadful thing.

"You must be out of your mind. It is your hide on the line, not mine. Help yourself."

Lion, slowly shook his head, solemnly resolved, to put as much space as he could between himself and that lion eating contraption.

With that, Jackal suitably delighted, bold as brass, strolled into the pen to retrieve a large juicy piece of meat. Then in a most audacious manner, lay down in front of Lion to eat it.

"How did you do that?"

Lion snarled, his eyes wide open in astonishment. Jackal turned to look back at the trap.

"Trap? That is no trap! I just proved it. I am eating the meat. I tried to tell you, but you were too overcome in your concern for eating this young man here. Although Lion, on second thoughts, as you correctly pointed out, you have a good fresh meal, waiting right here next to you. You can have him, while I finish the rest of the meat from that 'so-called trap' of yours."

"That meat was left for me, you thieving, impudent, slinking, little furball."

Anger overcame Lion, not taken to being insulted in such a manner, especially by a lessor carnivore like this peeving, flea-bitten Jackal. Lion, without a moment's thought, dived into that thing, grabbing the biggest piece for himself. At this, Jackal sprang forward, releasing the trapdoor, locking Lion inside once again.

All this time, Jabu had been praying for a miracle just like this one.

In a fit of rage, Lion spun around with a deafening roar as his paws hit the trapdoor. His roar was so loud, it was sure to have alerted the hunters from the village, for the second time that morning. Jabu knew they would come running.

Jackal, hearing the noise made by the hunters approaching ever closer, smartly disappeared into the bush with a firm grip on his handsome piece of meat. Jabu moving quickly, gathered the cattle, leaving Lion to his much-deserved judgment.

In the evening, when Jabu and his cattle arrived at the boma, Sipho was there bubbling with excitement, jabbering away while his friend shut the boma for the night. The overexcited Sipho was not making much sense, so Jabu motioned with his hand.

"Slow down, slow down. What is it, Sipho?"

"The lion Jabu. They have caught and killed a mighty lion. You and the cattle have missed all the excitement."

Jabu smiled at his long-time friend.

"We have had more than enough adventure for one day. Now I am going home to clean up and eat."

Sipho smiled, thinking to himself, what adventure? Then shaking his head, he ran back to the hunters, who once again told him the story of the huge mighty lion they snared and killed.

Jabu, eager to take a rest, rushed on home. Greeting his waiting mother at the door, haggard, he sat down, letting out a deep sigh. The day would come when he would tell his story.

The moral of the story, you say? There is a law that says, keep your word, even to your own hurt, because broken promises will always catch up with you. Even Lion, king of the beasts, was wrong and paid the price.

CHAPTER 24

HOW CHEETAH BECAME SO FAST

Long, long, ago somewhere in Africa, when all the people and animals were new. The Creator of all things decided to find out which of His animals was the swiftest of them all.

The Creator was fully aware of the fact Cheetah was the fastest of the animals with pads for feet, because he had made him so. And He was also aware the fastest animal with hooves from the antelope family was Tsessebe, the reason is, He created him this way.

Therefore, to find out which of the two fastest creatures was the fastest, would make that animal the fastest animal on the earth.

To this end, He devised a plan for Cheetah and Tsessebe to run a race against each other over a set distance.

Both contestants were informed of the pending race and told to get ready for the event for the first day of spring.

In those long-ago days, Cheetah had tender, soft paws and he realised although, for short-distance dashes, it was no matter. But this was going to be a long-distance race and he really wanted to win. Hatching a plan, he decided to contact Wild Dog, whom he knew had hard and strong paws, well suited to long-distance running because wild dogs are expert long-distance runners. Of course, any one of the animals were aware of this fact.

"Wild Dog, the Creator has arranged for Tsessebe and me to race against each other on a long-distance race to see who is the fastest of His creatures. The ones with hooves or the ones with paws. And my pads are only suited to short dashes, while yours are suited to long distance. This brings me to the reason I came here, can I borrow your pads for the race?"

"Of course, you can, after all, we are of the same family of padded paw animals and what is more, it would make me proud if you would beat a hoof studded animal like Tsessebe."

The deal done, they made the trade and Cheetah went straight off to train for the big day.

THE BIG RACE

WHEN THE SPRING DAY arrived, animals lined their way along the track, each one vying for the best spot. Some rooting for Cheetah and some for Tsessebe, but it was a great commotion indeed.

The race started from the base of a massive baobab tree on the side of a big plain dotted with thorn trees. The two contestants would speed down the plain, as fast as they could, to the hill on the far side. The first one to reach the hill would be the winner.

With the Creator Himself presiding from a high hill, Tsessebe and Cheetah lined up, and at His signal, down the plain like the wind itself they went, to shouts, snort, roars, trumpeting, barks, squeals, but it was a great rejoicing of encouragement.

Tsessebe soon drew to the front. To the assembled animals, he was so far ahead it appeared he would surely win. Suddenly, in a cloud of dust, the speeding antelope disappeared! Tsessebe had stumbled on a stone and crashed to the ground with an injured leg.

Soft-hearted Cheetah could not leave his rival lying in the dust all crumpled up. Instead of running past and winning the race, he stopped to help his competitor.

The Creator witnessing this was so moved by Cheetah's noble act, He bestowed upon him a legacy, making him the fastest animal on the whole earth. To equip Cheetah for his new gift, the Creator made for him paws, which were better, yet closely resembling those he had borrowed from his friend, Wild Dog.

Therefore, as it is to this day, Cheetahs, although of the cat family, have the paws of a dog, without retractable claws for climbing trees and clawing one another.

The moral of the story, you say? True nobility is always displayed in acts of kindness and generosity.

CHAPTER 25

LEOPARD, RAM AND JACKAL

Long, long, ago somewhere in Africa, when all the people and animals were new. Leopard was coming home from hunting one day when he came upon Ram.

"What is this, I see before me. A new creature. How strange."

Leopard had not ever laid eyes on such an animal of this type or colour before, which left Leopard somewhat perplexed. Causing him a little more apprehension than simply to muse to himself with regard to this strange new animal. Well, let us call it a new animal, from Leopards point of view, that is. We, - the people, - know Ram by the name of Oryx. Oryx live mainly in harsh semi-desert regions, but we will call him Ram for purposes of this folktale, to honour Ram for what he called himself. Ram was not totally restricted to deserts but visited his neighbours in the Savannah from time to time. On this day when Leopard met Ram, it was on just such a venture as this. Leopard had been hunting in his favourite Savannah haunts, straying too close to the desert on this ominous occasion.

So, we must excuse Leopard for being surprised to see such a tough animal in grey, black and white undertakers' apparel, sporting horns which went on forever, as straight as a die. Because Leopard had never seen such an animal as Ram before, he approached submissively, because tragically curiosity had got the best of him on this day.

"Good day, friend! What may your name be?"

The other in his deep gruff voice, - must be the desert air - beating his breast with his forefoot, declared.

"I am Ram. Who are you?"

"Leopard."

That was it, Leopard was out of there, taking straight off, homeward bound, more dead than alive from fright. Well, run he did, as fast as his legs would go. Putting as much space between him and that strange creature, as the bush and time would allow, hoping the stark memory would fade from his consciousness.

LEOPARD CONSULTS JACKAL

LEOPARDS LEGS KEPT going till they reached Jackal's place. Jackal lived not far from Leopard's place. As you can imagine, the two were familiar with one another, from a long time passed.

"Jackal, I am quite out of breath."

"I can see that. You also look like you got a big fright."

"Fright, what do mean fright, I am half dead with fright. And I am not ashamed to say that either. For I have just seen a terrible looking fellow, with a large thick head, attached are two long straight horns which go on forever. Then, when I asked him what his name was, he said gruffly in a deep voice, 'I am Ram' beating his chest with his forehoof. Without looking back, I ran for dear life, so here I am."

Jackal, shaking his head from side to side, was obviously not too impressed with Leopard's reactions, letting him know, in no uncertain terms.

"Ram! What a foolish fellow you are. That is a fine piece of meat you left behind Leopard. Never mind the tragedy. Maybe we can salvage your good find in some way or another. How far away is this Ram anyway?"

"He is far, near the big desert."

"Leopard, all is not lost, we shall go tomorrow to eat it together."

"Jackal, I know you are not out of your mind, but have you perhaps thought, maybe he has friends, many friends? Have you considered that?"

"I am not in the slightest worried, neither should you be. Till tomorrow then, meet you at your tree, early."

RAM'S WISE WIFE

IF LEOPARD SLEPT THAT night, it was not well, almost falling out of his tree a few times too many, dreaming he was being chased by a heard of Rams in undertakers' clothing. Too early in the morning, Jackal arrived at Leopards tree.

"Why so glum? You look like you had no sleep."

"I never."

"We are still going then, are we not?"

"Yes, of course, I am going. I take kindly to your judgement Jackal. You are wiser than most and a good friend, whom I respect."

Leopard leading the way, the two set off for the district of Ram. After travelling a fair distance, they came to a sandy dune covered with patchy grass and many short thorn trees dotted around in red sandy soil. The moment Leopard realised he had come to the spot where he saw Ram for the first time yesterday, he stopped, then slinking up the rise he peered over.

"There he is."

Ram, was wondering around scheming where to find some succulent provisions when he saw Leopard's head over the edge of the rise, then he saw Jackal with him. Immediately he went off to find his wife.

"I fear this is our last day, for Leopard and Jackal have come to eat us. What shall we do?"

"Do not be afraid, go out, take the child with you, then, when the moment is right nip it on the bottom, to make it cry as if it were hungry. Now listen carefully to my plan, then do exactly what I tell you."

Ram's wife gave him full instructions on what to do and what to say. Ram followed his wife's instructions to the letter, first going out with the youngster to wait for the accomplices to approach, pretending not to have seen them on the rise.

"See, there is one and a half of them already! Who knows how many by lunchtime!"

"We are not going to wait till lunchtime. We are going now."

Seeing Ram again was bad enough for Leopard, only this time there was one huge one with a smaller one, which caused Leopard's fear to override his trust in Jackal, he tried to turn back. But Jackal anticipated this, looping a leather thong over Leopard's neck, tying it fast to himself.

"Come on Leopard. Get up let us go eat him and the small one included. There are two of us and my teeth are sharp, are your claws up to scratch. Let me see. Ooo, yes, dangerous."

"All right, you better be right this time my friend. I am ready. Let us go.

As they approached Ram, Leopard slackened back. Jackal went ahead pulling on the thong tied to Leopard's neck, encouraging his friend not to be afraid. Jackal was holding tight on the thong around Leopard's neck as they came closer to Ram. It was then, when Ram put his wife's plan into action, shouting out in a loud voice while nipping his child on the rear end at the same time. Ram, rearing up high on his back legs, beat hard on his chest with one forefoot, booming out in his deep gruff voice.

"Look, son, we are saved, Jackal has brought us Leopard to eat. Our troubles are over. You can eat Jackal, for he is small and I will eat Leopard, for he is nicely fat."

LEOPARD'S STRAIGHTWAY HOME

WITH THESE DREADFUL, terrible words, Leopard, in spite of Jackals' pleadings to let him go, set off in the utmost terror!

Leopard ran and ran, yet worst of all, while he ran, he became more and more conscious, the faster he went, the closer he felt someone was chasing him. Dragging Jackal over hill, down gully, through vale, over rocks, through bush and brush, not once stopping to look behind him, till he brought back himself and half-dead Jackal, home again.

And that my friends, was how Ram escaped.

The moral of the story, you say? When someone calls your bluff, always do your best to keep your cool.

THE END

Mauritz Mostert © 2020

Don't miss out!

Visit the website below and you can sign up to receive emails whenever Mauritz Mostert publishes a new book. There's no charge and no obligation.

https://books2read.com/r/B-A-KVEF-LXLHB

BOOKS 2 READ

Connecting independent readers to independent writers.

Also by Mauritz Mostert

How The Leopard Got His Spots
Jabu And The Lion
How Giraffe Stretched His Neck
The Great Animal Battle
25 Famous African Folktales
How The Zebra Got His Stripes

Watch for more at https://wildmoz.com.

About the Publisher

Wildmoz is a dedicated African online book publisher, web magazine, committed to wildlife, culture and upbeat news on the ground. We publish the good stuff!

www.ingramcontent.com/pod-product-compliance
Lightning Source LLC
Chambersburg PA
CBHW030536030726
47495CB00004B/1016